Unfinished Thinking

An Insightful Novel

Unfinished Thinking

An Insightful Novel

DANIEL HILL ZAFREN

Published by Time Treasures Books, Goose Creek, South Carolina

ISBN 13: 978-0-9833042-4-1

Printed in the United States of America

Cover and interior design by Susan Newman Design Inc.

List of earlier captivating works by this highly respected author:

In a World We Never Made (2001)
A Door Never Opened (2003)
Shadow Selves (2005)
Network of Death (2006)
Not Lost – Just Not Found (2008)
Restless Beauty (2009)
Glimpses of Forgotten Dreams (2010)
Echo in the Heart (2011)
Double Hugs (2011)
Page Passage (2013)
Wish Winds (2014)

PART ONE

Thoughts –

Born and Raised

*Every man who has lived life to the full should,
by the time his senior years are reached, have
established a reserve inventory of unfinished thinking.*

— Clarence Randall

ONE

It would be difficult to pinpoint the exact time he became an EOM, an eccentric old man. It could have been when he stopped shaving and grew a full beard. It might have been when he no longer went for haircuts. It probably started at a really young age when he considered himself unlike others and was content to be an emotional loner. It just seemed so natural to shun what others pronounced as acceptable practices and normal behavior. It was certainly propelled when he quit his North Carolina State Government job in Raleigh at the age of forty-six and bought a rural store surrounded by trees that fronted on a highway in the mountains in the western part of the State. Actually, his transformation to the full blown person he was now was probably not due to a physical alteration of his being or life style but really just a state of mind. Even now at the age of seventy-two, Gillian Cooper believed himself to be a youthful spirit akin to the beatnik or hippie generations of the 1960s and 1970s. While others emerged from those compelling times to become something else, his psyche never abandoned that kind of life.

Eccentricity covers multiple antisocial patterns and within that to varying degrees. His personal rebellion not to conform to many societal expectancies was a far cry from those taking a disturbing stance or posture against staid institutions and other people who do not agree with their exaggerated agenda. He had always been and always would be a man of peace with a docile and introspective demeanor. His only threat to others was that he might fall asleep while they were speaking or during a lull in the conversation. He never married, although there had been opportunities and temptations.

He opened the store to be his own boss and to earn money without being part of corporate America. In the beginning, he carried jellies and jams obtained from local farmers as well as local craft items. The large wooden sign above the store read *GIL'S TRADING POST*. As his interest in antiques grew, he carried more and more of these items as he developed friendships and associations with other antiques dealers and so-called pickers who obtained items to sell to dealers as they roamed the region. Many antiques came with stories, real and imaginary, that he embellished as needed to make a sale. There was the classic story of a dealer who bought a bunch of boxes of old books at an estate sale and found an original Rembrandt rolled up in one of the boxes. Who has not heard of a person buying an item at a yard sale for a couple of dollars only to discover later that it was valuable even if hideous? One such story was the purchase of a white glass lamp for $10.00 that turned out to be a rare Tiffany lamp as Tiffany made very few white shade lamps. There were even humorous tales as the one where a dealer stumbled across an original and complete erector set to which he added a Viagra pill and labeled the item an erection set. As with his life-long practice of being an acute listener, there was usually much to learn by absorbing the knowledge others had attained through experience. A fascinating part of the antiques business is that one could spend a lifetime and not be an expert in all categories of antiques but it was always absorbing to find out new features and to acquire as much knowledge as one can.

After putting various antiques in front of the store or on the porch to attract passing motorists, he spent most of the time in the living quarters behind the store. The door to the shop was left open during the day. A bell attached to the front door of the shop would sound when the door was opened, although the first alert usually came from Andy, his nine-year-old German Shepherd. He had read that there was an art museum in France that had no human security guards and just guard dogs that roamed the halls and there had never been a theft or even an attempted theft. Andy was a sweet and loving animal, but he had an intense stare and imposing mannerism accompanied by an intimidating bark that left little doubt for a stranger that nothing should be attempted that he did not approve of. Gil relied on Andy's acute sense of smell and hearing, both features that had diminished considerably for him personally.

A set of rockers adorned the front porch of the store and Gillian often sat there with Andy at his feet. He would wave at the passing motorists, many obviously remarking to each other that there was a genuine mountain man sitting in the rocker. In the quiet moments, if he was not reading he would doze off or just let his mind wander to the limits it was prone to do. He tried not to search for regrets in his past life but rather to ingrain in his total being the satisfaction of being an EOM.

On good weather days, he would set out in part of the parking area some special antiques to entice people to stop. Selected popular items that people were tempted to buy included trunks, buckets, wagon wheels, and primitive signs. An old Coca-Cola machine that still worked was on the front porch and was a popular attraction, particularly during the warm months when parents would buy sodas for the children exclaiming their parents did the same when they were young. At times, young women would drive by, roll down a window and have fun with him with demeaning flirting remarks. They probably did not believe mountain men could have feelings.

An often-asked question by customers was where did he get all of the stuff? Of course, he oversimplified the response by saying they came from a variety of sources. Depending on the people, he would slant an explanation to bring out a laugh or a tear. Entertainment was part and parcel of the business.

The visitors were as varied as the antiques and ranged from novice to expert and from the curious to the know-it-all. Over the years he gained the knack of picking up quickly who they were and why they stopped. Occasionally, an attractive woman would enter the shop and that brought out a mixture of memories along with an emotional uplift. Andy especially liked folks with dogs as he rarely met a dog he did not like or get along with. Gil wished he could say the same thing about himself and other people. One overwhelming feature of an EOM is a distinct lack of patience and tolerance. There are just some people who have grating personalities.

The seasons brought different folks to the mountains. In the winter, it was mainly those headed to or from the ski slopes. In the spring, it was people bitten by wanderlust or to see the special mountain flowers. Some came to seek an unusual moss that only grows there and never needs watering. In the summer, cooler temperatures and mountain recreation such as river rafting enticed folks to flee from the cities. In the autumn, leaf peepers flocked to the scenic byways.

The great advantage of being in the same place for a long time was having made many friends. Not a day would pass when one or two would come by, sit in an adjoining rocker, and relaxed conversation would drift between any and all topics that stirred an interest. There was no demand for talk, and it would be comforting to even sit in silence with anther person who appreciated the significance of the pervasive quietness. A pot of coffee would be nearby, and Gil assigned antique cups to his constant visitors. Andy, of course, liked the friends best who brought their dogs with them for the visit.

Ruth Burns, who owned a small bakery in town, was a particularly special visitor. Ruth was a widow with three grown children who still lived in the area. They had dated at one point but it just did not blossom to an amorous union, although they became close as friends with an ongoing exchange of pleasantries and philosophical ideas. Ruth was well read and had a sharp and probing mind. Knowing full well that he had a raging sweet tooth, each visit she would bring a pastry or pie slice from the bakery along with a dog treat for Andy.

He rarely ventured out, and when he did it was in the old, beat-up truck he had seemingly forever. Andy loved to ride in the passenger seat. There would be the weekly jaunt to the supermarket and trips to auctions and estate sales. He had spent too many years cultivating a dull life. As far as he was concerned, eccentricity could range from unpredictable quirks to a total absence of quirks. One dear friend, a pastor at a local church, tried in vain to coax him to come and listen to his sermons. Gillian would not go because he did not believe in religion for himself. He was a moral and ethical man, and that was enough. He did not ever try to dissuade others who had a religious bent. After all, some needed and wanted that extra support to face what life had in store for them. His own rigid life let him turn his back on the practices and actions others deemed vital to their well being.

He was an early riser and needed only about six hours of sleep. Early morning was his favorite part of the day. It was as if the world was at his command. Few distractions dislodged his train of thought. Early morning brought a fresh look at where he had been and where he was going, even though it was all one and the same. For an EOM the great delusion is the grand scheme.

TWO

Gillian's childhood was a mind blur. He was born in Brooklyn, New York. His father was a quiet and hard working salesman who had little time to devote to the family, although he tried his best to set a good example for the children. He was considerate and affectionate with their mother and was quick to compliment her on ordinary life tasks. He was politically and socially liberal and had only a few true like-minded friends. Their mother was also restrained and loved to read to the children when she was not knitting or tending to household chores. Both parents were heavy smokers as so many of their peers were trying to emulate Hollywood idols, and both died from lung cancer four months apart in their early seventies. Gil never smoked but he was sure he had received enough second-hand smoke to adversely affect him. At times, catching a breath was difficult, almost as hard as catching a dream.

He had a brother, Alfred, who was three years older, and a sister, Frieda, two years younger. Alfred died of a heart attack in California in his early fifties, but his life had fallen apart before that when his teenaged son had committed suicide. He had been ridden with guilt over that tragic event, blaming himself in so many different and agonizing ways. In long telephone conversations, Gil had tried to ease his burden and to coax him to get professional help. Alfred refused to seek assistance to mend a shattered life. He died a broken man and was at the time of his death a janitor at a community center, a far cry from an earlier successful career as an architect. Whenever Gil thought about Alfred and the tortuous emotions that had gripped him, he would shake his head in a basic disbelief that it did not have to be that way, and it fortified the rewards of his own eccentricity.

His sister, Frieda, never married either, although it was not for a lack of suitors. She was attractive and vivacious. She still lived in Brooklyn in the same old neighborhood and ran a graphic design business from her home. Business was rarely consistent, but she managed to squeak out a living. She was also now entrenched in her way of life and was probably a comparable counterpart as an EOW, an eccentric old woman. They had not seen each other for many years although they did talk on the telephone every few weeks. Frieda loved to talk about their childhood, and he was not quite sure all of the events she related actually happened or an overactive imagination reached full flower in memory. She kept reminding him of how protective he had been. Then she would tell him a joke or two, and he would recite them to his rocking chair cronies as the latest offerings from the big city.

He had long ago forgotten the names and faces of childhood friends, although he did recall they hung out in the streets with no motivation or direction. He did become street wise if only through observing the comings and goings of others, and that distinct knack served him well throughout the years. He was a good judge of character and quick to sense actions of greed and deception.

They lived in a blue-collar neighborhood with families bunched together. Most people did not have a car and any travel was restricted to the subway and buses. There was no such a thing as a school bus, and he walked to an elementary school and took a city bus to high school and then to college. Their small apartment was on the third floor of an eight story building. It had one cramped elevator that usually was not working. The stairways were dark and a matchbook lobby was dismal and shabby. To this day he could not figure out how his father was financially able to send all of his children to Brooklyn College and then Alfred to graduate school. Gillian should have been a better student to reward the man's efforts, but even then the incubation of a free-spirited mind led him to do fully only what interested him.

Girls had been a puzzling mystery in those younger years. He was wary and shy in their presence. A basic inquisitiveness led him to want to know more about them. He befriended most of the girls on his block and the few in his building, and he was drawn more to the older girls. The one conclusion he made at the time that stuck with him was that young girls were as interested in sex as young boys were. The other feature that held true back then and was time-tested is that the better you know a person the more they are inclined to open up to you.

He would have loved to go away to college but it was not possible to go anywhere except to Brooklyn College. It had a limited campus life, although he transferred the curiosity he had in the small public library on the avenue in his neighborhood to the larger library at the college. He would roam through the aisles of books, the shelves crammed with tomes fat and skinny. To this day, he still wondered why some subjects evoked extensive thought and analysis while others were akin to a passing fancy.

It was at the college library that he met his first serious girl friend. In one of the book aisles, he had crouched down to look at a book on the bottom shelf that appeared so old that he was curious to know how it got there. Later on, he would recognize that most old things get relegated to the bottom shelf. Anyway, Annabelle Tucker had her nose in a book as she proceeded down that aisle and not seeing him tripped over his bent over form. Instead of being offended, she laughed. That put him at ease immediately, and as he reached out to disentangle their bodies his hand went right under her blouse that had pulled out from her skirt and it rested on a naked breast. In the effort to right themselves, her hand pushed against his aroused groin. They both laughed uncontrollably.

To distinguish himself from most others who called her Anna, he addressed her as Belle. She reciprocated by calling him Lian. They would study together at the college library, and he became a much better student. She was a book enthusiast and would, at times, be so engrossed in what she was reading she would not hear what he was saying. They went to the movies every Friday night, and then would make passionate love in the small basement beneath her family's modest two-family house. That home was only four blocks from his apartment building, and that is one of the mysteries of city living that people can live just a few blocks apart for many years and never saw each other before. Strange how things do not happen. The other lesson he took with him was that life, especially the chance at a different kind of life, could be right under your nose.

A year later, a certain monotony had set in and the couple gradually drifted in different directions. A parting kiss has a different kind of meaning than a first kiss and is equally significant.

He wondered what had happened to Belle. Perhaps, she had gone on to do great deeds. Too bad he did not believe in computers. He had been told you can track down people that way. Part of his eccentricity was the belief in letting sleeping dogs lay. Andy agreed with that too.

THREE

In his senior year, he just happened to be in the college administration building when the North Carolina recruiter was there taking applications for various state jobs in Raleigh. Half-heartedly, he listened to the recruiter's pitch and picked up the accompanying literature and application form. He did not have the slightest idea what he wanted to do after graduation or of what value the liberal arts degree was or might be.

The more he studied the job literature, an administrative position on the State Planning Commission seemed like a good launching place to survey his own future. Moving to a different geographical location with fresh experiences also had a certain appeal for a life wanderer.

It was not until his application was accepted and he moved to Raleigh did he fully realize this was the South. Segregation was contrary to his beliefs fashioned by both the liberal teachings of his father and growing up in a place where cultures and races intermingled freely. Under the Civil Rights Act of 1964, all overt aspects of segregation waned although existing mindsets might never fully accept change.

For the first year, he rented a small apartment within walking distance of the job just to make sure things would be to his liking. Once he decided to stay, with the money he saved from a year's salary he was able to put a down payment on a small house on a wooded lot on the outskirts of the city as well as on a car. The house had been built in the 1940s, and it had a charm and attractiveness that was appealing to one who never lived in a house before. It was actually described as a bungalow. Furnishings were obtained from visits to the large flea market held at the fairgrounds every weekend. Nothing matched, but that was of no concern to him.

He adopted his first German Shepard at the pound, a six-year old named Flash that apparently nobody else wanted and was shortly due to be euthanized. They bonded immediately, and he was sure that Flash knew that Gillian had saved him. Flash was content to sleep the day away in comfort on the old sofa. Before and after work, they took long walks and Flash delighted in all of the smells of freedom, a characteristic that Gil echoed. He also loved to ride in the car. Gillian took it hard when Flash's peaceful life ended four years later. No matter how many dogs one has over the years, it never gets any easier when the pet is lost.

One of the fringe benefits at the job was the bevy of young women who came to Raleigh for secretarial positions or to be in the typing pool. On nice days, he would invite one of them to join him for lunch in the park adjoining the office building. They would get sandwiches and engage in light-hearted and at times animated conversation. The more interesting women he would ask to lunch numerous times, and he dated a few of them that had special qualities. He made friends of them all, and that created a friendly atmosphere which made for an easier work environment, another life lesson absorbed and remembered.

The flowering from the seeds of his eccentricity, perhaps better described as the growth spurt of a free spirit, came as the hippie generation took over pop culture. Campus demonstrations, love-ins, street-corner bearded musicians and poets, and he felt a rising impetus to break away. That came eventually when he left the job and headed for the mountains. Even before he settled in to his niche there, he was convinced such a move was right for him. He never doubted the correctness of that decision or tried to second-guess his future. The meandering free spirit had found a contented resting place. It was for all intents and purposes the uninhibited evolution of his eccentricity.

One of the women he had dated often, Amanda Fowler, offered to go with him when his plans were developed. He was sure she had marriage in mind. It was a tempting situation because he did like her. She was a warm and giving person with a quick wit. Yet, he believed her to be too rational, too predictable to be a constant companion. There was no doubt she was hurt deeply by his refusal to take her with him. Another life lesson he prescribed for himself – avoid hurting others when possible.

As with Belle, there were times he wondered what had become of Amanda. Did she ever think about him and whether the mountain dream was realized? Can you ever think kindly of those who have hurt you? Does a hurt provide new resolve and fortitude or does it just add a bitter ingredient to the formula of life?

There had been another woman that he had some serious feelings for. She was an administrator and attended many meetings with him. He had admired the way she challenged archaic or unrealistic ideas. Danielle Marquest was a French exchange student and attended a local college in the evenings. They went on some unusual dates as she shunned conventional dating places and ideas. She taught him to ride a bicycle, and they hiked through much of the countryside. Some of the trails were precarious, and she delighted in difficult challenges. He very well might have agreed to take her with him when he left if the opportunity was there. She, of course, was bound to her job and classes as part of her foreign exchange program, and she constantly talked about a man back in France that she had an attachment to.

He used the profit from the sale of the bungalow to buy the store. So, all in all the job stint had served a practical purpose besides allowing his erratic personality to mushroom. That was another lesson to ponder about. One should capitalize on every life situation to develop and nurture the wherewithall to venture out to new pathways.

The main thing he carried with him from Raleigh, in addition to the German Shepard he had acquired, SLY, was a burgeoning book library and an accompanying thirst for reading. Belle would have been proud of him. He had picked up so many books at the flea market that most were stored in boxes as his scant bookshelves could not house them all. He doubted he could ever read them all in his lifetime, but such was a noble idea. Even now he could not pass up a bargain book or one that captured his interest. He probably should heed what an antiques friend once told him on a day he bought a contraption that he had no idea what it was or what it might be used for. She had pronounced matter-of-factly, "It is not a bargain if you do not need it."

FOUR

It was a warm day for May. He was sitting in a rocker with half a cup of coffee in his hand. Ruth had just left, and the taste of the peach pound cake she had brought with her for him to savor lingered in his mouth. As he was prone to do, he rehashed their discussion in his mind, trying desperately to put forth a stronger position than he had done at the time to her suggestion that he was getting too old to live out here alone and that he should move into town. He was not alone. Andy looked after him and there is no substitute for the comfort of familiar surroundings. Sure, the winters were brutal and business was slow. The howling frigid winds kept him indoors most of the time. He had the over abundance of books to pass the time and the wood stove to keep him toasty. Andy would spread out before the stove and would not budge except for food and to take care of his business. Gil had bantered that he would not leave this place until his beard and hair turned all gray. By some quirk, there were only flecks of gray in both.

The strain of thinking of points to bolster his position and the satisfaction of the peach pound cake led him to doze off. As he did so, he spilled the half cup of coffee in his lap. It was no longer hot but soaked through his overalls and he bolted out of the rocker. Andy barked at the quick movement as well as at the car that screeched to a stop in front of them.

The woman who got out from behind the wheel of the dark blue Lexus was immaculately dressed in a black suit with light brown hair up on her head in a bun with not a strand out of place. He guessed her to be in her forties, but it was not easy to tell a woman's age these days.

She was not beautiful but did have finely etched features that made her attractive and alluring. The high heels were another tip off that this was not a country woman.

She approached him keeping a wary eye on Andy who could care less. She looked in Gil's eyes and then her eyes dropped to the large wet spot in his lap. "Couldn't hold it in?" A chuckle was interspersed between the mellow tones.

"It's coffee, not piss. Care to smell my crotch?"

"Crude as well as rude, I see."

"That's what folks get when they jump to conclusions."

"It is perfectly alright if you were excited to see me. After all, when we were born we need diapers and when we get old we need them again. It is the full cycle of life."

"You are right. I am excited to see you. I promised my dog, Andy, some fresh meat and you showed up on cue."

"You sure are a disagreeable fellow."

"At your service, ma'am."

She moved closer to him and motioned to the rocker next to the one he had been sitting in. "May I?"

"It is ten dollars an hour or any part thereof."

She sat, crossing a shapely leg. "Put it on my account."

"On account you are not going to pay me."

"Hey, you are smarter than you look."

"If you are trying to ingratiate yourself to me, you are taking the wrong tact."

"You use some big words for a mountain man. I bet there is an interesting story behind that gruff exterior."

"That's fifty dollars an hour or any part thereof." He sat down and sensed that this was going to be a long conversation. It was already enjoyable. He liked a feisty woman. "What are you really after?"

"I want to marry you, unless you are already married."

"Out of luck, lass. Never been married and never will be. I have too much sense for that."

"Are you gay?"

"Yes. I am happy being unhitched and free to roam and choose which female I will have a roll in the hay with."

"How much do you charge for that?"

"City women are half price because the quality is lacking."

"I am running up a big bill here, I can see that. Is it that obvious I am from the city?"

"Is it ever!"

"Wow. I am impressed and I think we are in for a long talk."

"I reiterate, what do you want besides imposing on my peaceful life?"

"I was enjoying the banter. I guess it is time to be serious. I am from the Board of Health and I have come here to condemn this rat hole."

"Andy ate the last inspector. Are you sure you do not want to change your story?"

"O.K., you win. My name is Connie Crawford. I am a reporter at the Charlotte Observer, and I would like to do a series of articles on the attraction of the mountains for city people. I came to spend a few days to get material and take some pictures. I saw your store and thought it might be a good place to start."

"Your lucky day, lass. This is the best place to start alright. Your husband doesn't mind you wandering alone on uncharted seas where monsters lurk?" He noticed she did not have a wedding ring on, but that does not necessarily mean she is unmarried. Some married couples shun that practice.

"I never had a husband. I have yet to find a man who can hold my interest long enough for me to want to be with him. Besides, I wouldn't have asked you to marry me if I was already married." She made a mental note that it certainly was true that one cannot tell a book by its cover.

They talked for the entire day. Adorned by fresh overalls, he made them lunch that they ate while sitting out on the rockers. She asked him a torrent of questions about the mountains, the antiques, and his personal life. She watched and envied him and his knowledge as he aptly handled the few customers that came by. She particularly liked the leather-bound books housed in the living quarters. She volunteered information about herself as well. She was fifty-seven years old, had lived in Charlotte all of her life except for the period when she went to college in Ohio to get a journalism degree. She was an only child. Her parents were deceased, and she had lived on the forty-second floor of a high rise condominium for the past twenty years. She was a stranger to country life as any perpetual cliff dweller might be. She was quick to admit she did not know what she had limited experience with. This included mountain men, or as she now called them monsters of uncharted seas.

He made a simple dinner, mainly roasting fresh vegetables that one of his farmer friends had brought to him. She ate with gusto as they sat at the small table near the now inactive wood stove. She admitted she did not know how to cook and ate nearly all of her meals at restaurants. A home-cooked meal was a special treat. He could count on one hand the times he had eaten at a restaurant in the last ten years.

When they had finished the meal, they sat again outside, a cool breeze accentuating the quiet evening. There was little traffic on the dark highway at night. She would remember the peacefulness of such moments, such a stark contrast to the sounds of city living. He put one of his flannel shirts around her shoulders, and an earthy smell was added to her new-found experience.

Few surprises loomed in his life, but one certainly arrived when she offered in a whisper, "May I stay the night?"

It took a moment for him to respond, a rarity for his usually quick mind. "You already know there is only one bed. At my age, snuggling and cuddling are my only specialties."

"That sounds grand to a tired woman. How much do you charge for that?"

"Since it is really for me, it is free."

FIVE

He made scrambled eggs and toast for breakfast as she showered. She came to the table wearing only the flannel shirt he had draped around her the night before and she had no makeup on. Her hair, now down, was long and full. She looked younger than her years, and there was no denying the glow on her cheeks.

It was only after breakfast when she had dressed and drove off to town as the next step on her trip that he felt a letdown. After all, it had been a long time, perhaps too long, since he had received and had given affection.

He turned towards Andy. "Yes, my dear friend, that was one special woman!"

Andy barked twice, as if he was saying, "I sure agree with that. Too bad she didn't have a dog."

Connie called him on her cell phone when she arrived in town. He knew what a cell phone was but never could quite grasp the reason or the need for one. "I know you were worried as any sea monster would be, so I wanted to let you know I am here in one piece."

"That is kind of you."

"The town is quaint, so I think I will enjoy poking around. I also wanted to thank you for yesterday and last night. They were among the best of times in my sheltered life. I never would have guessed that on the first step of my trip I would discover a gold mine. I keep saying there are no surprises in life, but meeting and being with you was a delightful surprise. I never kissed a man with a beard before, a long beard at that. The thought before yesterday might have repulsed me.

Can you imagine, I never even noticed the beard? Mountain men may be one of our greatest national treasures."

"Thank you for your sentiments, but I think you did more for me than I did for you."

"I doubt that."

"Anyway, it is the mountain air. It can do wonders."

"Then I must find a way to bottle it and take it back home with me."

"That has been tried many times. It doesn't work that way. The magic lies only in being here."

"Shucks! In any case, thank you for waiving all of my expenses and thank you for giving me some warm and lasting memories. I mean every word."

"Likewise, lass."

"Take care, mountain man."

"Be well and be safe, city slicker."

He held on to the telephone for a moment before putting it down, as if that might be a way of holding on to the significance of it all. A long sigh said his farewell.

In the afternoon, his friend of many years, Len Glassman, stopped for a visit. Len brought with him his mixed breed dog, Day Break, so Andy was excited. The two dogs got along very well. Some six years earlier Len had been driving along the old mountain railroad grade road just as the sun was coming up on a winter's day. A scruffy dog was in the road shivering. The dog was friendly and let Len put him in the cab of the truck. Len took him home, fed him, and gave him a bath. The dog had no collar or tags, and since he was so friendly Len figured it was someone's pet. The veterinarian checked him out and guessed he was about two-years old, and also thought he was a pet since he had been neutered. Len put up a dog found notice in the doctor's office and other places, but no one ever responded or were there any notices of a matching lost dog. Thus, the two became buddies, and Len named him after the event at the time of their meeting.

Len had learned carpentry from his father. He did not finish high school and supported himself with odd jobs and working part time at the hardware store. He just happened to be working there when Gil came in shortly after moving. Gil asked him if he knew someone who could put up some shelves for him. Len's beaming response was, "You are lookin' at the best."

That was the beginning of a tight friendship. Having no fixit skills of his own, Gillian much appreciated Len's constant manual expertise. He marveled at the meticulous work Len exhibited. The store looked inviting with the shelves lining the walls, and Len put a series of shelves for books in the living quarters. Len gasped as Gil unpacked the books. He had never seen so many books in one place before. Len had a keen sense of country humor and a genuine homespun philosophy. The many intimate conversations they had over the years were enjoyable for both men. Len had married a local girl early on, but three years later she left him to go to Florida, taking their infant daughter with her. He had not heard from either once since.

Len was in a rocker and Gil poured him a cup of coffee. "I had a special visitor yesterday."

"Do tell."

"A gal from the city, a reporter, who is doing a series of articles on us folks. When she saw yours truly sitting here, she couldn't keep away."

"Do tell."

"She stayed all day."

"Do tell."

"She stayed all night."

"You crazy loon! I almost believed you up to that point."

"It's all true."

"Maybe, Ruth is right. You have been living alone so long you have flipped."

"You live alone."

"Yeah, but I live in the real world. You live so close to your books and this old junk you can't tell the difference between fact and fiction."

"You are an old coot! It really happened."

"You have any proof?"

"No."

"Did Andy bite her?"

"No. Andy liked her."

"Yeah. Yeah. Any woman who got that close to you and ole Andy would have had her for supper."

"You don 't have to believe me."

"Not to worry, I don't. Wanting something to happen don't make it so."

Gillian grew silent. Did he imagine it? Could it be that he was losing his mind? No, it was real. It was too good not to be real. It sure would help if Andy could talk. "Believe what you want."

"I always do. Someone has to keep you straight. I ain't goin' to believe everything you say even if you are smarter than me. Never have, never will."

"Same here, you toothless wonder."

"That's why we are friends. We know each other real good."

Len and Day Break left after Len finished the coffee. A couple of customers came by and Gil made one good sale. Before going in for supper, he rocked for a bit. Others might doubt him, but he always had a firm grasp on what he saw and what he heard. He thanked the streets of Brooklyn for that. Connie was real. He was sure of that. Or, was he?

SIX

A similar scenario played out two days later when another old friend, Gary Yearling, stopped by to chat. His yellow lab, Junior, jumped out of the truck first and trotted off with Andy into the woods behind the store.

Gary was some thirty years younger than Gil. He was a plumber and worked for a large plumbing contractor in the next county. He was usually on call in this county so the company let him keep the business truck all the time. He had a cranky and unpleasant wife, and it was a relief for him to be busy with numerous service calls. He stopped to see Gillian whenever he was in this part of the county. They had met when Gary was working as a volunteer at the election polling station, and he had an abiding interest in old stuff so that when he came across something he thought Gil might be interested in, he brought it to him.

Gary parked himself in an adjoining rocker and sighed. "Seems like I never stop long enough to catch my breath. Maybe I should open a junk shop right across the highway and be glued to a rocker like you."

"You couldn't sit still for ten minutes even if you wanted to."

"You'd be surprised."

"I would."

"Then, how much would you pay me not to open a competing store?"

"Nothing. I thrive on competition. You can buy this store if you want to. Ruth thinks I should move into town."

"That'll never happen. You wouldn't last a week in town."

"You know it. I know it. She knows it, too."

"Anyway, Mary would never let me do anything that is risky."

"Don't get me started on that subject. You need and deserve a different kind of woman."

"Look who is talking? You are far from an expert on women. When was the last time you made love to a woman? I bet it was in the last century."

"You might be surprised."

"I am your psychiatrist, so don't hold back on me."

"And what makes you my shrink?"

"I keep your pipes clean, don't I?"

"I guess that is as good a qualification as any."

"So, spill the beans."

"And clog another pipe?"

"I won't charge you for a service call."

Gillian had not intended to tell anyone else about Connie since the response had been one of disbelief from Len. But, it came out anyway, perhaps because talking about it was a form of reliving it. A real psychiatrist would have a field day with that!

Gary was silent for a moment, almost as if he expected more of the story. "I know you are a schemer and a dreamer, but I think you have outdone yourself this time."

"Len had the same reaction."

"There is, you know, a vast difference between credible and incredible. I hope when I get to be an old coot like you I will have retained some sense of reality."

"Don't you mean if you get to be my age? I kill those who doubt my word."

"No wonder the population of the county is dwindling. Nearly everyone does not believe your stories. Just remember, they won't let you take Andy with you to the slammer."

"Just be glad they let you take Junior in the company truck. Mary would have eliminated him by now."

"Speaking of Junior, I better get him and get going. I don't get paid listening to fairy tales." He whistled and in a short time Junior and Andy came around the side of the building.

Gil came to the side of the truck as they got in. "Next time stay for some coffee so I can tell you the same story. Since there won't be any variation in the events, maybe then you will believe it all happened."

"Hey, Buddy, I don't doubt you believe it is the truth. It is just that we know you better and can see this clearer than you can."

"I am going to take back what I paid you."

"Too late," he said as the truck pulled away. "I've already spent it on an order of truth serum for you."

SEVEN

More than just the local folks were his friends. Those who came to the mountains regularly, be it for weekends or for weeks at a time either in cabins they owned or rented, would stop by for a look and for conversation. One such couple, an elderly couple, the husband a retired professor at Wake Forest University, Lawrence, and his wife, Cybil, did not have a cabin but had a trailer they parked permanently at the camp grounds. They were knowledgable about antiques but had no room in the trailer or any available space in their small Winston-Salem home. What he especially liked about the Professor and Cybil was that they both were entering a phase of eccentricity. Each time they would visit, he would show them any new items in the store and then they would have long discussions, often highly emotionally charged, on subjects controversial and important to old people, such as the scandalous cost and quality of health care, government waste of taxpayer money, inconsistent foreign policy, and the disturbing indifference of young people to the elderly and the very world around them. A feature of their personalities that Gillian admired was their willingness to utter their unabashed opinions without concern over their acceptability or popularity. They were folks after his own heart.

A middle-aged lesbian couple were also frequent visitors on their way to or from a small cabin they had on the river where they loved to canoe. Leslie Graff and Harriet Wilkens had been a couple since the early volatile days when the concept of gay couples stirred strong opposition. Both had good jobs in Charlotte and were unrestrained in showing their inclination even if uncomfortable consequences followed. They were interested in antiques but knew little about them. They trusted Gillian's expertise and he guided them slowly to an enjoyable collecting experience. They had two Yorkshire terriers and Andy was gentle with them even as he towered above them. They would lie together and Andy would wait until the little ones fell asleep before he would close his eyes.

Leslie and Harriet would have numerous stories of the events in the gay community. They were good-natured and sincere in their appreciation for what he did for them. Gil looked at sexual orientation as a personal matter. It was not his place to judge it or to let it interfere with a person's other qualities. Harriet was a gourmet cook, and she would usually bring him a tidbit from a recent creation before the trip to the mountains. Often he was not sure what he was eating, but there was no denying it was delicious. Harriet would feign forgetfulness about the ingredients, assuming correctly that it could well scare off an old man who craved the simple life.

Then there was Larry Evans, a young stockbroker in Rock Hill, South Carolina, who had a condominium in the mountains. He considered himself quite a lady's man, and would come to the mountains each time with a different young attractive woman. He would stop at the trading post to show his potential conquest a mountain man and brag about his knowledge of antiques. He would buy the woman a small trinket and would receive a warm hug in return. Gil knew there would be a small sale on each visit, and gazing upon a young and beautiful woman was still a treat. It would take a high degree of self control to keep his mouth closed. Maybe the residual protective instinct he apparently had with his sister added to his discomfort. He had heard and read that old people can be as gullible as youngsters, although he was sure he was not among those ranks. The elders, if they relied upon their experience, should know better. But, he had seen it many times, no matter what the age one can be taken advantage of. Especially is this the case when a clever and disarming person is the prime mover.

Gil liked it when the families came by more than once. The children, who may have been reserved on the first visit particularly with Andy, now knew the dog was no threat but a delightful play invitation and the scary old man just a gentle soul with fascinating stories to be told. After they would leave, there were times he wondered what he might have missed not having children. He probably would have been an attentive parent, but he surmised that there was more to it than that. Patience had never been one of his virtues, and at this point in his life's journey it was a struggle to be patient even with himself. People go through life knowing that there are aspects they missed out on. As they round the final bend, one should not look back. One can only wonder what it might have been like doing this or that differently. Even that mental vision is often hazy. It also detracts from the present moment which might command full concentration. He wondered if Connie regretted not having children.

EIGHT

Validation of Connie's existence, and perhaps his own as well, came ten days later in a manilla envelope that Gerber, the local postman, brought with the electric bill. It was an article from the newspaper, carefully excised from the whole paper. There was a picture of Gil and Andy on the porch of the store with the trading post sign clearly visible. The caption read: Secret Treasures. The article, detailed and well-written could only have resulted from an extended personal visit.

Len's response when he was shown the article was as Gil would have predicted. "O.K., she is real and was here. Doesn't prove more than that."

Gary's response was more gentle. "I guess I did not give you the credit you deserved. I believe you now, but if she was such a prize why did you let her get away?"

Ruth stopped by with two pieces of peach pie, one for now and one for him to enjoy later. She sipped on the coffee he had handed her in the cup he reserved for her because it had a baker's hat on it. She settled into a rocker and patted him on the arm. "You make the best java. I could use you at the bakery."

"Thank you for my slice of the pie."

"Have you thought any more about moving into town?"

"No."

"Abe Gosser has closed his hobby shop because he is not well. He and his wife are moving to Florida. It is smaller than this place, but would make a nice antique shop. There is shelving on all of the walls. You could find a place in town to live within walking distance of the shop. Best of all, as you already know, the hobby shop is just a few doors down from the bakery. It will be convenient to keep you saturated in sweets."

"And lose my girlish figure?"

"At your age, that should be the most of your worries."

"You are a dear lady, without a doubt, to be concerned about me. Don't get me wrong. I am grateful. It is just I am not yet ready to give up everything I enjoy about being out here."

"What is that? Being alone?"

"In a sense, yes. I can rule this kingdom without regard of neighbors or protocol. Here, even the quiet communicates with me."

"You are as crazy as a loon."

"You know me well and a good point. You don't want a crazy man being a few doors away from you, do you?"

"I'm the only one who can keep tabs on you. Maybe the only one who wants to."

"Too big a job for a little lady. I'll tell you what," he had an urge to placate her, "I will think about it." He added to himself, "But, not much."

They rocked in unison for a few moments before she spoke again. "An old man can't fool an old lady. You're just hoping I'll go away."

He chuckled. "Not in the least. You are among my favorites, and while it may not always sound that way, I appreciate your concern."

"It is from the heart. You and I may have missed our time in the sun, but I have a special feeling for you."

"Likewise, fair lady. You are a really good person and, you may not believe this, I take everything you say or do in earnest. I don't know what is becoming of the world with hatred and violence overtaking civility, so the gentle and loving people like you deserve admiration."

"It is frightening what is going on. In a way, I feel protected here distanced from city violence and terrorism, but that may be a false security. There just are too many bad people, too many nut cases on the loose. Hey, that's another reason for you to move into town. You can protect me and my business. I'll reward you with extra goodies."

"You won't give up, will you?"

"No. You'll see the logic in it and, hopefully, before your health gives way and you have to be in town."

"Strange that you say that about my health. I talked on the phone last night with my sister in Brooklyn. Out of the blue, she said that if I ever needed looking after I can move in with her. Did you two conspire against me? Do you two know something I don't know?"

"You know better than that." She leaned over and kissed him on the cheek. "I better get back. Folks coming home from work will want desserts."

After Ruth left, Gil stayed in the rocker with Andy snuggling by his feet. He never had a health issue, but that was not to say one could develop even over night. But, he would handle it as he did everything else......when and if it happened. He had seen and heard of too many people getting hung up on what might happen. That was a different sort of eccentricity, a personally destructive kind. The famous saying by Alfred E. Neuman from Mad Magazine popped into his head: "What, me worry?"

NINE

Several people mentioned the newspaper article when they stopped to browse through the store. Gil tried telephoning Connie several times to tell her some increased traffic was due to the article. Each time he had to leave a message. It was her cell phone that she had with her all of the time, and his number must have shown up on the phone's display, so he finally figured she did not want to talk to him and he quit calling. She probably considered it a fling inherent in the article hunt and either quickly forgot all about it or in recalling it was embarrassed to have been with him. What he did not know was that Connie was afraid to answer his calls, afraid to let any emotional distraction disturb her staid existence. It was best left as a journalistic incident. There was no way city could meet country with any lasting result to her benefit. The last thing she needed was an emotional entanglement. As an intellectual person she knew that made no sense, but it had to be that way in her small world. In spite of the calls, she had a feeling that Gil looked at it the same way. A person spends too many years getting entrenched in a comfort zone to break free. It is amazing how almost anything can be rationalized away.

Ronnie Gibbons was one of his more intellectual and socially liberal friends. Ronnie was a transplant to the mountains from Florida where it was too hot and buggy for him and his wife, Yolanda. Ronnie had an advanced degree in philosophy, although his career had been with the Justice Department in Washington. He had met Yolanda during one of the Civil Rights marches on Washington when she was a librarian in a small Maryland town just outside of Washington. There was an instant attraction, and in two months she quit her job and moved in with him when living together without being married was still frowned upon. He liked to tell the story about the first pasta meal she made for him when the pasta was woefully undercooked and the sauce she used was a can of Campbell's tomato soup. He described it as a marvelous experience. They married three weeks later. They had two daughters, both now teachers in Virginia, and each summer they would visit the old folks in the mountains with their families for extended vacations.

Undoubtedly, due to his stint at the Department of Justice and his super liberal leaning, Ronnie was constantly on the hunt for causes to espouse. He had sucked Gillian into quite a few of them over the years, many fizzling out or getting to a point where they really did not know what they were doing or fully understanding what they were all about. Ronnie was a firm believer that the only way you can be at peace with yourself was to do battle for others. Yolanda was more of a silent partner. She kept notes on all of the undertakings, filling a scrapbook of the endeavors.

Ronnie parked himself in a rocker as Yolanda went into the store to check for new additions. His husky voice was tinged with authority. "Yes, my friend, those fools in Washington just keep wasting our money. These foreign escapades cost us dearly in money and in the lives of those who fight them who should not be killed or maimed but leading productive lives on the home front. We are antagonizing other nations meddling in their affairs and giving fuel to fanatic groups to conspire against us and seek revenge. I feel sorry for my grandchildren growing up in this kind of world. I am not even sure the world will be here when they grow up."

"You missed your chance to change things when you were in Washington."

"I really did not see the total picture back then. Of course, I wielded no power whatsoever."

"Need I remind you of the old saying that a million feet can wear down a mountain?"

"Need I remind you how difficult it is to get a million feet to march to the same drummer?"

"Need I remind you that someone has to lead the way?"

Ronnie grumbled or snorted. Gil was not sure which exhale it was. "So, this is how two old men talk."

"That's half the battle. Now to get young people to listen."

"If I knew that I would be retired in Monte Carlo and not in the Appalachians."

Just then Yolanda came out carrying three cups of coffee. "All of this discourse must make you thirsty. If I had a dollar for each time you talk about saving the world, I could fund the Social Security System. Have some coffee and take a nap. That is as productive as you will get."

"Sage advice, doctor Yolanda," Gil proclaimed.

She turned to him and spoke after handing him a cup, "I like that music box with the horse on it. Our granddaughter, Sadie, would love it. She is taking riding lessons and is enchanted by horses. What tune does it play?"

"Lara's Theme from Dr. Zhivago. Actually, describing it as a music box is not technically correct. A music box is a carton of music. This is a musical box."

"See, you learn something every day. How much is it?"

"It is yours as a token of friendship."

"Nice of you, but I cannot accept it unless you keep Ronnie in return."

"That's no bargain! Do you know what you get when you rub two old men together?"

"You keep old women away."

"Close. You get two old men who have been rubbed together with no purpose or result. Keeping him is your burden."

"Would you sell him in the store?"

"Won't bring much. Take the musical box instead."

She bent down and kissed him on the cheek. "You won't make any money giving things away. If all eccentric men were like you there would be no eccentric bachelors."

TEN

All of the autumnal signs pointed to a harsh winter ahead. The deer had changed color early from a golden hue to a dark brown. An abundance of acorns littered roadways and trails. Wooly bears were plentiful and one of the earliest frosts on record descended on the valleys. Gil made numerous trips into the woods with a chainsaw to stockpile wood for the stove which he covered and tied-down with a tarp to keep relatively dry.

A large number of leaf peepers had stopped at the store, thanks in part to the series of articles Connie had written as well as a vibrant leaf color display as the product of a wet summer. The extra money should tide him over through his variation of a winter hibernation.

Ruth tried again to get him to come to town even if just for the winter months as a trial. She was not surprised that he would not agree to budge from his domain. She knew how stubborn he was, a quality that was part and parcel of his personality. She even tried a form of bribery by saying that she would not drive out to see him and bring a treat if there was snow or ice on the roads, but he could help himself daily at the bakery if he were in town. That ploy was unsuccessful.

The first snow came a week later. It was wind driven and created blizzard conditions as the drifts kept getting higher. Gil and Andy camped out before the stoked wood stove, the howling wind causing the boards of the house to creak. Many might find such an isolating event disturbing, but he was comfortable in moments that were totally his own. He had yet to experience the malady associated with old age where memories are disconnected and disconcerting. He rather enjoyed languishing in the capture of his past and partaking in one of his captivating mind games where an outcome might have changed if he had done something different. It was also reassuring to recall moments and experiences from long ago even if the details were not always crystal clear.

For all of his shyness around and wariness about girls when he was in elementary school, there had been one absorbing adventure revolving around a girl that came to mind at moments when he was immersed in recollection. Even though it was totally one-sided, it left a lasting imprint on his makeup. Sheila Davenport, and it amazed him that he could still remember her name after so many years, lived at the end of his block but it might have been in another world. She was a grade ahead of him and he was never sure whether she ignored him on purpose or if she was just not aware he existed. Yet, he was enraptured by her and spellbound when she was nearby. He was transfixed by the freckles, the long straight auburn hair, and the shapely legs visible above the bobby socks to the short skirts she wore. He would follow behind as she walked home from school with her friends. An outgoing personality brought flashing smiles and a quick laugh to her being. He never dared to approach her even at the rare times she was alone. It was his first obsession, and his waking thoughts and dreams merged into fantasies of a youthful devotion to an idea or a spirit if he could tell the difference even now. He was sure many children have deep imaginary experiences, and such aids in the development of the scope and breadth of feelings and sensitivities.

At the end of a school year, Sheila and her family moved to Long Island. He was probably the last one on the block to find out and he had figured since he had not seen her that she was away for the summer. His emotions were so intense that he often would see a girl in the distance and he was sure it was Sheila. Over the years he would point to that example to show that imagination can be deceptive especially as it filters in to dreams and early memories. His current friends would joke with him that he needed a full time psychiatrist. Eccentricity capped by early emotional sensations such as with Sheila probably provided a greater accuracy to that diagnosis than they fully realized.

He should have used his sister to get close to Sheila. He could have had her befriend the admired figure, and at the very least she would have been unable to deny his existence. Another mystery of life – why does cleverness often come too late?

The telephone disrupted the introspection. Ruth's voice was distinctive as it was familiar. "Buried yet?"

"Getting there."

"Are you okay?"

"Sure enough. I could use a warm pastry, but I'll manage."

"I am waiting for you to come to your senses. Pastry is just one of the rewards."

"You need to realize that wallowing in one's own misery is reward enough."

"If I really thought you believed that, I would leave you alone. I know you get great pleasure in yanking my chain."

"I suppose that makes you a yankee."

"Very funny. I am going to be a constant pest."

"What do you mean going to be? You already are a pain in my ass."

"Pain is good. It proves you are alive."

"I'll give you that. Mail me some pastry."

"Mail me your common sense. Wait, you can't mail what you don't have."

"Common sense is overrated. Stubborn is the in thing."

"Beecher once said that the difference between perseverance and stubbornness is the will and the won't. You have perfected stubbornness because you won't do anything, especially if it is for your own good. Pig-headed may be a more apt description."

"Oink."

"I am glad you admit it. A few more storms like this and then I'll tell you where you can shove your oinks. Keep safe and warm you old buzzard."

"Likewise you old witch."

"I love you, you know."

"I know, and I love you, too."

After they hung up, he guessed there was a tear in her eye. Once again his imagination might have predicted a reality.

ELEVEN

To keep the well and pipes from freezing up during exceptionally cold weather, the old mountain trick is to keep a faucet dripping during the night hours. There is usually enough water usage during the day to keep the water flowing. A city person would probably find this incredulous. Yet, even pipes in city houses can freeze and burst during extreme cold, particularly if the pipes are on an outside wall.

The shop was not heated. Most antiques can withstand extremes in temperature, but to err on the side of caution, certain items that had moving parts, such as clocks, were brought into the living quarters. He turned off the toilet in the public rest room and put RV antifreeze in the tank and bowl. He well remembered an early winter when he had a small refrigerator in the store. The cold permeated to the inside and cans of soda exploded. Experience is a good teacher, although the best teacher is the experience of others where one does not actually have to endure the mistake and hardship. Precautions and remedies of others were stored in the arsenal of tips for daily living.

He received a telephone call from Jack Cheshire, a dealer friend in Wilkesboro. Gil had met Jack early on at a large antiques festival in Virginia. They became friends right away and would often bump into each other at events. Jack was an interesting fellow with many years of experience in the antiques business. He was also in his seventies and was presently living with his fifth wife. He talked about his wives as he did about his antiques. In fact, after each divorce that wife was classified as an antique. The marriages came easily as Jack was handsome and a charming talker. All of the divorces were amicable and it just seemed that each of the ladies could not handle the competition with his consuming interest in antiques, especially as it led him to travel to any place at the hint of a special deal.

Jack called him whenever he came across an interesting story, and Gil would reciprocate if he heard of one. This time, he had heard of a dealer who bought from a farmer a Page shotgun with Clark Gable's name on it in gold. The farmer had it squirreled away in an old barn. The dealer gave him $24,000 for it, and before the week was out he had resold it for $75,000. Gil shook his head in amazement.

Jack would also impart things that he had recently learned from others about the mystifying world of antiques. He shared Gillian's theory of learning whenever and whatever he could.

Gil reiterated the premise that each day something was learned was a good day. Since there was so much to learn, there was often a string of good days. Of course, at his ripe old age it was another thing to remember all that he learned. But, you have to know it before you can forget it. Some truisms are eccentric by their very nature. The more thought-provoking the truism the more he enjoyed espousing it.

> *By my rambling digressions I perceive myself*
> *to be growing old.*

> — Benjamin Franklin

There were days on end when the telephone did not ring. Today was a busy day. Fifteen minutes after hanging up with Jack, the telephone rang. Gil answered the telephone in different ways, often with the humor which most of his callers expected. "You pulled me out of the shower, this better be good."

"Were you in the shower alone?" The voice of his sister, Frieda, was easy to place.

"It is unsanitary to shower with others. Everyone knows or should know that."

"Only to save water. We need to protect the environment in any way we can. I saw on television that there was a bunch of snow your way. I thought I better check on you."

"I'd prefer if you sent me a check, but I'm fine and actually like being snowbound. There is no way anyone can get around to bother me."

"Even ten feet of snow here in Brooklyn would not stop people from going out."

"That is why you have bragging rights."

"Don't you mean bragging wrongs?"

"All bragging is wrong. No snow there yet?"

"It has been cold but no snow. Remember how I used to tag along when you shoveled walks for a dollar?"

"The problem back then was that you did not have any friends of your own. That is why you were always bothering me."

"Shoot me for loving my big brother."

"That might have worked."

"You loved every minute of it. Your sister idolized you and I still do."

"Your idolizing is out of whack."

"Are you calling me whacky?"

"If the shoe fits, wear it."

"It runs in the family."

"No argument there."

There was a moment of silence before she spoke again. Her voice was more subdued. "I had another reason for calling."

Voice and mannerism can be a prediction of what follows. He knew the humor had ended. "I'm listening."

"I guess there is no way to say this than to just say it. I have colon cancer. It is in an advanced stage. I ignored early warning signs because I am obstinate and cheap. I have no health insurance. I have six months to a year, perhaps longer if I start chemo. I can't afford that and don't believe anyway in prolonging life unless it adds to the quality. Without quality of life I do not want to live. All I want to do is for them to give me something to ease the pain as that gets worse, which they say it will."

She hesitated, and he took that as his cue to speak. "My dear sister, is there anything I can do? Would you like to come here so I can look after you?"

A sob intermingled with a form of chuckle. "Just what I thought you would say. I wanted you to know because I love you. I need to be here close to my doctor and in familiar surroundings. I am most at ease here. I have a couple of close friends who will be here for me. But, I would like to see you before I die. There is nothing like a final hug in person. I know you are entrenched there and this is asking a great deal from you."

"Nonsense," he exclaimed. "I'll come just as soon as there is a break in the weather."

"No. No. In the spring will be good. I might be less presentable then, but I am sure I will have enough strength to hug you."

"I will come now, just as soon as I can get out and make arrangements here."

Another moment of silence. "That's love, alright."

"Yes, it is."

The arrangements were easy enough to make. The old truck was not up to make such a trip, but he could borrow Gary's car since he used the plumbing truck most of the time. Also, Mary had a car if they needed to get around. Ruth offered her car, but Gil knew she needed it for the bakery needs. Len would look after Andy at his place, and he would be good company for Day Break. Gil would secure the store as best as possible, turn off the water in the living quarters and just hope all would be well. Gary would check on the place whenever he was over that way. Now, only if the weather would cooperate.

TWELVE

Three days later the temperature rose and sunny skies prevailed. He set out for Brooklyn trying to brace himself for whatever he might find there. Eccentricity does not prepare one for the unknown.

It was a long trip to another world. He scarcely believed it was the same place he had spent so many early years. The streets were narrower and the buildings crammed together closer than he remembered There was even so little familiarity that recollections seemed far removed from reality. Not even the presence of Sheila or Belle would have calmed his restless spirit. He was out of place here. Only focusing on his reason for being there brought a sense of calm.

His heart sank when he saw how ghastly Frieda looked. An extremely pale complexion surrounded sunken cheeks and eyes with dark circles around them. She could not rise from the bed to give him a hug but managed to wrap her arms around him with some force. She only released her hold when it evidently became too much of a strain for her.

Frieda's best friend since high school, Naomi Bernstein, was with her almost constantly. She answered the door when Gil knocked and grabbed his arm with a knowing tug. Upon seeing her, he did remember the short and shy girl with long black hair and wide black eyes. She was now stocky and the black hair while still long was now flecked with gray. He even recalled upon seeing her that her voice had been squeaky and that had changed over the years to a husky tone. She lived alone in the same building and was a retired librarian at the county library. She had never married, declaring that she followed Frieda's practice of going it alone and never found a Jewish boy worthy of her mind and body.

Frieda had a small one bedroom apartment. A narrow kitchen led to a tiny dinette. The living room was a good size but was nearly completely taken over by two massive tables upon which two computers and all sorts of graphic design materials were spread out. Naomi had borrowed a cot for Gil to sleep on and it was cramped between one of the tables and the wall. A bunch of copies of lithographs of abstracts were hung on the walls which probably only the original artist knew their resemblance to reality or their significance. Paintings was another area where Gil always was attentive to learn more. Value varied all over the field with an artist's reputation more of gauge than the painting itself. When asked, he advised people to buy or collect what they like and not be overly concerned with the concept of an investment.

After Naomi left, Gil sat by Frieda's bed holding her hand. Her eyes were closed but she was not sleeping. It was a form of contentment that lessened her discomfort for the moment. He closed his eyes and let the silence speak for itself.

When she opened her eyes she stared at the loving face that had been such a vital part of her early life. Her voice was raspy and he strained to hear her. "It means so much to me that you are here. Just to see you brings a rush of warm memories that settle in my heart."

"I wish the memories can work a miracle."

"I take what I can get."

"That is a better thought."

"Speaking of memories, there is a large box by the long table in the living room filled with family pictures and other things from our past. I want you to have it and to take back with you."

"Sure."

"I don't believe in Heaven or in any form of after life. Even if I did, I don't think it would make dying any easier. But, just in case I am wrong, is there anything you want me to tell Alfred?"

Even in her condition, she still retained a sense of humor. "Tell him he missed the family reunion."

"We never really did talk about his ending."

"Perhaps, it was all better left unsaid. I tried to get him to agree to professional help. I felt useless much as I do right now."

"Not true. You are doing so much for me by being here. As for Alfred, there is no way to gauge what we did or did not do for him. I tried to help him but he was his own worst enemy. I remember him as a boy, and he always tried to be tough but he was a softie, sensitive and insecure. He did not have our resiliency. Maybe he inherited that weakness and it was passed on to his son."

"I never considered it that way, although it makes sense. We'll never really know."

"I am not sure anything makes sense anymore. I should have made a better life for myself, perhaps going elsewhere and doing something for humanity. It is too late for hindsight, too late for regrets."

"I am not sure that is the right way to look at it. Home is where we are and not where it might have been. It is not a place or an accomplishment. It is a state of mind."

Her hand had gone limp and she had gone to sleep. He was not sure she had heard him or if he should have even said anything. As usual, there is often more meaning in the listening than in the speaking. He closed his eyes and weariness led him to a deep sleep. Sleep is a robber but death is the greatest thief.

THIRTEEN

Over the next three days, Frieda slept most of the time. The pain medication had been increased in strength and frequency. Gil stayed close by and Naomi was there most of the time. They had extended conversations while Frieda slept.

Since Naomi was a librarian, they talked at great length about books, authors, and collections. She lived in the same building and took him to her apartment where floor to ceiling bookcases housed hundreds of books. She lent him a couple of books to read during the many quiet times. She knew very little about the world of antiques and was curious enough to ask him some pointed questions.

Naomi was an only child in a poor orthodox Jewish family and had lived in Brooklyn her entire life. Her parents died when she was in her early twenties and had to shift for herself. Her vivid childhood fantasies, such as an all-consuming belief in fairies, led her to read whatever she could get her hands on. Becoming a librarian was a natural offshoot. Through the world of books she maintained an increasing distance from serious reality. Since she was the caretaker of her parents through their terminal diseases, she wanted to be with Frieda as much as possible to give her comfort and support in the final days. No demand was too much of a hardship for their friendship. They had become friends in high school, and over these many years that friendship endured to soothe otherwise lonely lives. Every Saturday they would have lunch at the Jewish deli on the avenue, and every Wednesday night they would share dinner together at the Chinese restaurant down the block. Frieda had talked about Gil so often that Naomi felt she already knew him. At times, she wondered if her life would have been any different if she had an older brother.

Naomi was sure that she had restricted her romantic and marital options by dating only Jewish boys. There had been no serious involvements and no marriage proposals, a difficult life path for a woman who was basically a romantic thanks to her reading habits and for one who wanted children. She found Gillian interesting, and it was too bad he was not Jewish. Maybe, at a different time and at a different place it might not have mattered, but one does not wander from a life-long emotional commitment in the autumn of that life. Although as an intellectual challenge perhaps one should change before that life is over. She had shunned the normal concerns of life and thinking, and her old age would not be what she might make it but what it had been made for her. For all of the audacity she showed to other things she surrendered to the mediocrity of her own being. She could accept that but would not be able to explain it if pressed to do so. As an activist for all causes affecting animals and people, she could do and wanted to do for others that which she was unwilling and unable to do for herself. A tragedy of old age is when regrets supplant dreams. That commonality made the friendship with Frieda that much stronger.

Two days later, Gil started back to North Carolina. Naomi promised to keep him posted on developments, and he would return when the end was imminent.

Saying good-bye to Frieda was difficult, and her crying tore at his heart. She knew he had to go and actually did not want to hold him back. She also wanted to spare him from seeing any further deterioration of her condition. Yet, part of her wanted to hold close to the past to bolster what little future she had left. She hugged him with all the strength she had. One easing feature settled in her mind. When her heart stopped, it would be full.

Unfinished Thinking

FOURTEEN

Arriving back in the mountains it was cold but dry. Gil and Andy had an elated reunion, both realizing that this had been their longest separation by far. The car was returned to Gary, and it was a good thing he was there to drive them to the store because Mary would not have let Andy in her car.

After getting the wood stove going, as the place quickly warmed up he called Frieda and spoke with Naomi to find out how things were there. Then he called Ruth to fill her in on developments. He unpacked his small travel bag, and as the night settled in with cold winds he fed Andy and then had a bowl of soup. Physically tired and emotionally drained, he crawled into bed. Before he fell asleep a fleeting thought entered his mind of how nice it would be to have Connie's warm body to hold. Andy was sprawled out before the stove as his world was righted.

It snowed heavily during the night. The winds had subsided and the snow covered everything. Unlike the city where snows turn to an ugly dirty slush, the mountains retain a pristine white snow condition as another reflection of the pure mountain air and natural surroundings.

He puttered around a bit going through the motions with his mind elsewhere. A totally pensive mood encased him. Perhaps, the ordeal and full significance of Frieda's plight were settling in.

From his arm chair by the stove he could see out of a side window. A bird, a beautiful male cardinal, was perched on top of the old fence that ran along that side of the building. Why would a bird hang around in these conditions when he could have flown south for the winter? Some birds do stay all year and he was vigilant about putting out seed all through the year so he could enjoy their beauty, antics, and love songs. He put out scraps for the deer too whenever he had something they might enjoy. Perhaps, as Gil mulled it over, a reason for the bird to stay put was that he still had things to do. He related it to his own situation of why he stayed here at the store. It was more than just the comfort and independence factors. There was a smoldering idea that he still had things to do. As he surveyed his life, it had been replete with satisfying accomplishments and to his self-established agenda there had been no action or reasonable dream unfulfilled. Never having a constant female partner or children were failures of a sort, but that was just how it happened to turn out. Even if he wanted that to be otherwise, that opportunity was gone and he was not sure he was any worse off. In old age one needs to accept what cannot be changed and to affirm that a meaningful life still exists.

If there is nothing left to be done as far as the stops on life's highway are concerned, does that mean a resignation that life is or should be over? What else could there be to do? There must be an area not fully accounted for, an undertaking that remains to be completed. It has to be in the realm of thoughts. It has to be unfinished thinking. That means that in an analysis of his being he was not yet fully the person he was meant to be or wanted to be. That meant that for all of the years dedicated to establishing his form of eccentricity, as well as all of the intent and motivation dedicated to that endeavor, the process was not yet complete. Was he not as eccentric as he professed to be? Was there something beyond that eccentricity? Would he be able to figure that out or would he be on his own deathbed still puzzled by who he was? This even assumed that his thoughts could reach a conclusion. What if all thinking is unfinished?

Immersing himself in such an intellectual maze was disconcerting. He had to accept the fact that he was not the person he thought he knew so well. There was more to solve the puzzle, more to define the boundaries of his being. It seemed so inconsistent with the professed maturity of old age to doubt oneself. Uncertainty and mystery were for youngsters. And yet, unfinished thinking may be what keeps us alive until the end.

By the afternoon the bird was still perched on the fence. Gil was on the fence as well.

FIFTEEN

By the next day the roads were passable. Gil and Andy drove to town. He mailed the check to Naomi that he promised to help with Frieda's expenses. There went the money he thought would ease his way over the winter, but it was more important to do this. He was accustomed to scrimping as there had been many lean times. There still was the possibility that some sales could come along, and that would surely help.

He stopped at the bakery. Ruth did not expect him. "You look terrible."

"I don't feel too chipper. Travel and compassion take much from the spirit of an old fart."

"It would affect anyone."

"I sure could use a sweet fix."

"Just what I was guessing. Go behind the counter and help yourself while I go in the back and get a dog treat for Andy."

He waited until she returned. It just did not seem right for him to pig out on his own, although that was an appealing idea. "I prefer that you pick out a morsel for me as you know what is stale and you need to get rid of."

"Very funny. How about a piece of humble pie?"

"Not my first choice."

"Alright. Here is an almond danish that came out of the oven ten minutes ago. Have a seat and I'll get you some coffee."

Just a few small tables lined one wall. Most folks took the goodies out. As he sat, he bent over and gave Andy the treat which the perceptive dog knew was coming.

Ruth sat across from him with a cup of coffee of her own. "I need a break anyway, and entertaining you is a public service. Is there any change with Frieda?"

"I talked a bit with her this morning. She is weak and has no appetite, but her frame of mind appears good considering what she is going through. The medicine keeps the pain in check."

"She is fortunate to have a good friend close and a good brother in the wings."

"For sure, nothing replaces a good friend. That is why I am glad I have you. You are sweeter than your sweets."

"Flattery will get you everywhere. I suppose you want another piece for now besides the one I will send home with you."

"A friend even knows what you are thinking."

"Some things are truly obvious."

"Speaking about thinking, do you think more now than when you were younger? Is your thinking finished?"

"Whoa, big fella. You are changing horses on me here. What brought this on, and what do you mean?"

"Since I came back, I am taking a new look at myself and I am having trouble placing thoughts in the larger picture. Are all of your thoughts done? Do you get new ones? Do you ever feel you have not thought something all the way through?"

"You are getting too serious on me. I am not sure I can handle that part of you. I am just a simple woman and I go out of my way not to get involved in complex situations because I know it can be troubling or hurtful to try and get out of them. But, if you are asking me if I have afterthoughts, I have them all of the time. I second guess myself constantly."

"I suppose that is part of it."

"I have always known you are strange, but I declare you get weirder all the time."

"I suppose seeing someone die brings out a form of weirdness as it leads you to ponder on many philosophical levels."

"That's too deep for a person tying to figure out whether a cake should have one or two layers of filling."

He grimaced as if a bolt of pain had shot through his body. "What do you believe tomorrow will bring?"

"Besides better weather and more customers, whatever it brings I'll just accept it and make the best out of it that I can."

"My basic philosophy, too. But, perhaps, it deserves another look."

"Simple is best. Let's all keep things that way so at least we have that in common."

"Makes sense. I better get going. If a customer came along that would go a long way in simplifying my life."

He hugged her and gave her a kiss on her cheek. He put the extra danish on the dash board so that he and Andy could stare at it all the way home.

The bird was not on the fence. Did he do his thinking on the fence or did he just rest there and go elsewhere to do thinking?

Maybe Ruth was right. He was not only eccentric but also weird.

SIXTEEN

The days passed slowly. A few people stopped at the store, but they were just tire kickers and he had the feeling there was more interest in why a crazy old man would keep his business open in the dead of winter.

Len and Gary stopped by for brief visits. Pressing duties held them back from staying long, and each had the feeling that Gil was preoccupied with his sister's illness as his mood was sombre and he did not talk much. They had no clue that it was really something else. The premise of unfinished thinking had taken a stranglehold on his outlook and was bogging him down. He suspected that the only person who might be able to capsulize the issue and refine it into a recognizable whole was the professor. At least, he might know more about if birds think. As an elder scholar, the concept of unfinished thinking might even be something he encountered before in the annals of academia or even within his own frame of reference. The professor would probably not be up until late in the spring as their trailer was not heated. He could telephone him, but Gil knew that this subject would be best explored in a face-to-face discussion.

He was not going to mention this troubling mental anguish to Naomi, but it slipped out in one of their conversations. Besides talking during the day when he called Frieda, Naomi began telephoning him in the evenings when she returned to her apartment for a break. These conversations grew more open and involved. Naomi confessed that she was troubled as of late with the concept that her life should take a different turn. She had not labeled it as unfinished thinking although that was another way to describe it. From a placid and predictable life as a librarian, with an emotional replica in her retirement, an increasing urge gnawed at her to break away from the mold she had been in. A call to a new beginning is the way she described it. Rather than accepting the life she had made, or rather the life that was there and that she fell into, being with Frieda and watching her die the notion became stronger that in a way right now she was living a form of death and it was a shackle that she needed to break free from. The more they talked about it, and the more she pondered over it, the stronger she embraced the concept of unfinished thinking.

Both scoured their book collections for tidbits to reveal that others had wrestled with the dilemma. That would be fuel to add to the mental fire. That common mission drew them closer. Either their standards were ill defined or their books primarily involved other avenues of wisdom because the results of the search were scant.

Our thoughts are epochs in our lives, all else is but a journal of the winds that blow while we are here.

— Henry David Thoreau

Thinking is the talking of the soul with itself.

— Plato

To him whose elastic and vigorous thought keeps pace with the sun, the day is a perpetual morning.

— Henry David Thoreau

The world we have created is a product of our thinking, it cannot be changed without changing our thinking.

— Albert Einstein

All sorts of reflections of this nature passed through my mind — for as I grow older I regret to say that a detestable habit of thinking seems to be getting a hold of me . . .

— H. Ridel Haggard

Sometimes I think and other times I am.

— Paul Variete

The thoughts that come often unsought, and, as it were, drop into the mind, are commonly the most valuable of any we have.

— John Locke

At the end of one of these intense discussions, he blurted out, "Now you know why I am an eccentric old man!"

She shouted out her response. "You can see that I am quickly becoming an eccentric old woman!"

SEVENTEEN

Over the next several days the bird appeared at random times. When he perched on the fence he would stay for a few hours. He would be motionless and Gil could not tell whether his eyes were open. Was his mind open? Whenever Gil dozed his mind did not turn off, Now that he had much to think about, was it possible to think too much? One thing became clear, the more one thinks about something does not necessarily mean it brings answers. Perhaps, the process was more important than deriving at answers.

Ronnie stopped by for a visit. He would be a good person to discuss the thinking quagmire with until there was the opportunity to talk with the professor. Ronnie's high intelligence would be useful in the probe.

They sat by the wood stove each holding a cup of freshly brewed coffee. After relaxing for a few minutes, Gil cleared his throat. "The visit to my dying sister has upset my usually staid outlook."

Ronnie offered an interrupting remark as an invitation to continue. "The specter of death is a mirror in which we see ourselves."

"I am totally perplexed by the concept of thinking, not just the process but in the sense that, all of a sudden, my thinking is unfinished."

"Ah, interesting. In this day and age when computers do most of our thinking for many people thinking has not even begun. In the time of the great thinkers there were few distractions so ideas could flow easily. I dare say, their best thoughts were the ones that opened the way for further thinking. So, it is not illogical to say that all thinking was and still is unfinished. On a personal level, it can mean many things it seems to me. For example, you realize you have more to learn. You may want or need to change the way you live so that there can be more satisfaction in what you do and accomplish. Or, it could mean you are merely aware that something is missing in what you do or in who you are. Or, it might just mean here that you haven't thought about death and the situation with your sister ushers in the compulsion to think about your own death. Too many of us do not want to think about death because it is an upsetting subject."

"All well and good, but say I feel something all of a sudden is missing from my life or I am not sure I am who I am. How do I know what is missing? Even if I can hurdle that obstacle, where do I look to find what is missing? Or, if I am no longer satisfied with my life as it is, at my age and in my financial condition what are the possibilities?"

"I am not the answer man, for sure. But, we all probably doubt ourselves at some point in life. It is more common in the young years, but once the spigot of self-doubt is opened it is very difficult to turn it off."

"You're not much help."

"Ah, you struck the right chord. I cannot live your life for you, nobody should do that. You need to solve your own problems, find your right direction. It is your demon to wrestle with."

Gil was quiet for a moment. "I suppose what bothers me the most is that I have been content or, at least, satisfied with my life for a long time. I hate to have that shattered."

"If that were true, you would not have the reaction you are having. With all of your doubt, it is too late to step backwards. However, you may, as far as I can tell, find that your past is your future."

"That would be coming full circle. I think the mystery is more complex than that."

"Could be. Stay tuned."

"Could be may be as good as it gets."

"Could be."

EIGHTEEN

Over the next several weeks, it became apparent that Frieda's condition was deteriorating. Her voice was weaker and the conversations were brief. He dreaded the announcement that came one night that Freida was slipping away. Naomi was of the opinion that there would be little to gain if he came, but she knew Gil would make a decision on his own. He had concluded all along that when her death was imminent he had to be with Frieda for her and for himself.

He was able to make the same arrangements when the roads were clear. Andy was dropped at Len's, and while content Gil could almost read the dog's mind, "Here we go again." Gary had the oil changed in the car and it was ready to go. Ruth gave him a bunch of pastries to nibble on.

When he arrived in Brooklyn, Frieda was still hanging on almost as if she knew he was coming and wanted to wait. She gave him a slight smile, and he held her hand as he sat by the bed. Naomi stood behind him with her hands on his shoulders. Frieda closed her eyes for the last time.

Naomi handed him the note that Frieda had dictated to her the day before.

> *Gillian, you have been the treasure in my life. Be happy for you as well as for me. Remember me with love.*

The only sounds in the room were Naomi's sobs and his own heavy breathing. He rarely cried, not because he thought crying was a weakness but because he prided himself in believing he absorbed all emotions in the anticipation of what was about to happen. Now, the tears came freely as he held the limp hand. It was a forever goodbye.

Naomi had already arranged for the cremation, and the service came for the body shortly after being notified of the demise. It took only a small carton for them to pack Frieda's personal items. They moved the cot Gil had been sleeping on to Naomi's apartment. An auctioneer came the next day and emptied out the remaining contents of the apartment.

On the evening before Gil was to return to North Carolina, Naomi prepared a simple meal for them. They sat at her small dining room table without engaging in the enjoyable dialogue they had been accustomed to. Naomi had given careful thought to what she was about to ask him. It represented a major upheaval from the pattern and scope of her life. Yet, there was no way she could deny the clarity of the vision it presented and she would speak her piece no matter the consequences. Frieda's death scared her as she related it to her own being. She had nothing to look forward to and would eventually die in this place alone. She was not able to and, in fact, did not want to deny the growing feeling she had about Gil. She was comfortable with him, and they shared a basic compatibility based on their mutual interest in books and the unrestricted confines of their personalities. For a woman who had never experienced love, this had to be as close to that sensation as she would ever get. The fact that he was not Jewish was not even a factor. With that long beard he could easily be a rabbi.

"Gillian," she began slowly as she stared into his sad eyes, "I have a big favor to ask of you."

He caught her gaze and there was a degree of intensity in her voice even as the words were spoken so slowly. "I'm listening."

"Good. You don't have to answer immediately if you want to think about it." A deep breath fortified her resolve. "Bluntly, I want to go back with you."

He did not say anything. He recalled Amanda's urging in Raleigh to go with him when he announced his intention to go to the mountains. He also remembered the lesson he learned as a result to avoid hurting someone if it was at all possible. Actually, Naomi's request did not come as an unwelcome surprise. She was plump and not nearly as attractive as Connie, but he sensed the rambunctious urgings that matched his own, and he liked being with her and talking about various subjects. He knew people, and he was sure that Naomi was good-natured and genuine in her thoughts and expressions. Perhaps, Ronnie was right in the sense that his unfinished thinking was, at least in part, that he needed to alter the course of his life. Maybe it was time for him not to be alone. A compatible person as a companion might be the right direction to go. He reached for her hand and liked the way she intertwined her fingers with his. "I would like that."

"We are both set in our ways, I know that. I may hate the country. But, I do like you. Maybe, we can try it for a few weeks and see what happens."

"Fair enough." He pulled her up from the seat and they embraced. The sensation of body against body was pleasant. She smelled of the mountains, clean and pungent. They held each other for a few minutes, reluctant to break apart. If they were writing a book, and living life is in so many ways like writing a book, it was time for a new chapter.

NINETEEN

They went directly to the store. Gil started the wood stove and showed Naomi around while the place warmed up. It was just what Naomi was hoping it would be. Everything peaked her interest, especially the many books.

Gil went to pick up Andy and then to return the car. Len shook his head in disbelief. Just when he had thought he had seen it all, Gil did the totally unexpected. Gil had either gone off the deep end or this woman must be something exceptional. Len leaned towards the first conclusion, but he would withhold a final determination until he met this woman. He wondered if he might have to pay her off to get her to leave. Gary was home when Gil arrived there, and then Gary drove Gil and Andy back. There, he met Naomi and he liked her right away although he did not know what to think all the way to the store. Naomi was pleasant and friendly, qualities lacking in Mary, so he was easy to win over. He also had a life-long attraction to plump women, so that was an endearing feature. Perhaps, it was time for him to leave Mary and move on with his life just as Gil had now done.

Naomi and Andy greeted each other as old friends. She had never had a dog, but she loved animals and had been active in many animal causes. She recognized immediately that Andy was a special dog, and Andy behaved as if there was room for his allegiance to more than just Gil. Andy was not sure whether this woman was another Connie or something more, but he concentrated as he always did on the here and now. He particularly liked the way this woman scratched him behind his ears and the butt rub was a bonus. The more people around the better.

Gil made sure the old truck started up and then headed for town to get groceries and to tell Ruth the news. It sure came as a surprise to her. Bringing a woman home was totally out of character for Gil and this was just another weird act. There was a twinge of jealousy as she had been the number one woman in Gil's life even though there was no love interest. What bothered her the most was that this completely undermined her case that he should move to town because he was alone. Other than that, she would withhold any further judgment until she met the woman.

While Gil was gone, Naomi put away the things she had brought with her in the dresser drawer Gil had cleared for her and in the closet. She did some cleaning and then sat by the wood stove with Andy lying close by. She looked out the window and saw a beautiful bird sitting on the fence. She took that as a sign that even nature was welcoming her, and she sighed in contentment. She sensed she had made a good decision and that she would be happy here. She probably should have taken risks at earlier stages of her life, but that was then and this was now.

When Gil returned, he guided Naomi through the contents of the shop. She was fascinated by the variety of items, many of which she had never seen before and had no idea what they may have been used for. Gil explained that antiques, contrary to many contemporary items which are solely decorative, as old materials they had a specific use and in some cases multiple uses. She was also amazed at Gil's knowledge of the inventory. After a first look at the book collection, she suggested she rearrange them by genre. Gil thought that was a mighty good idea.

Naomi cooked a simple supper with some of the groceries Gil had returned with. They ate by the stove and then read for awhile. They would glance at one another, and a smile and thoughtful remark would follow.

When they retired in the narrow bed, Naomi wished she were slimmer so there would be more room. But, holding a warm body close in the night chill was reward enough. It further accentuated for Naomi what she had been missing her entire life. For Gil, while he was still convinced his thinking was as yet unfinished, he had reached a new plateau. The loner instinct was gone. Now, it had become vital for his well being to share his life with this woman. She was a composite of all of the earlier love interests in his life.

The next day when Naomi started her book project, she came across a saying that she read aloud. It profoundly expressed what they both were feeling.

Every heart sings a song, incomplete,
incomplete until another heart whispers
back.

— Plato

PART TWO

Thoughts

Maturing

TWENTY

Naomi held a festive party to celebrate Gillian's seventy-seventh birthday. It had turned out to be a good investment in many ways that they used Naomi's savings to have Len construct an addition to both the shop and living quarters. The shop could now accommodate pieces of furniture and the living quarters easily house all of Naomi's books as well as there being a separate large bedroom with a double bed in it. The smaller living quarters would never have been able to hold all of the friends that came to mark the occasion.

When the building was enlarged, it was decided to expand only on one side so that the old fence on the other side could be preserved. After all, it was the bird's favorite perch, his thinking post. The bird had come to symbolize not only the thinking process and nature accepting Naomi's presence but also as an icon of their solidarity. The bird represented the beautiful life they had together.

After the guests left, Naomi insisted that Gil sit out on a rocker while she cleaned up. She knew he would pursue his quest to finish thinking about something or someone before he dozed off. It had not taken her long to know him well because it was basically a reflection of herself.

Gil rocked gently as Morgan and Molly, the brother and sister German Shepherds adopted from the shelter two years ago after Andy died, lay at his feet. Andy's passing was not the only downward emotional spiral over the past five years. The professor died shortly after Gil and Naomi had a series of discussions with him and Cybil about thinking. Then, Ruth had a lengthy sustained serious illness with a slow recovery period. She and Naomi had become close friends, and Naomi helped Ruth's children to care for her as well as to run the bakery until she was back in charge.

Sweet moments came as love flourished. Meaningful moments were showered with affection, new and welcome sensations for those who had not frequented that type of world before. It spilled over to the caring for and running the business. It was enjoyable doing the tasks together, and business kept improving. Naomi had a creative touch for displaying the items, and she convinced Gil that a clean antique would sell better than a dirty one. His argument that dust and grime reflected true age was considerably weakened by many instances where dirty items were passed over for sales of cleaner ones. In fact, some antiques he had for a long time soon sold after being cleaned.

Naomi joined him on the porch. Gil's eyes opened. "Done already?"

"You've been asleep for an hour."

"Not sleeping, my dear, finishing a thought."

"The professor said no thought is ever truly finished."

"Correction. Finished for the moment. By the way, Cybil looked terrible, didn't she?"

"Yes, but when she lost Lawrence she lost her world. Fortunately, there are children and grandchildren to fill some of the emptiness." A cold chill ran along her spine as she thought there would be little to fill her emptiness if she lost Gillian.

"She is selling the trailer. She'll stay in Winston-Salem. There are too many memories in each place."

"Memories are like thoughts. There can be not enough or too many, and they are never finished either."

"We relive memories as we do thoughts. A memory is a special kind of thought."

They were silent for a moment. Molly nuzzled her chin on Naomi's knee. "We have had our share of good memories over these five years. Now that we are as one, I am not sure I can handle losing you. I still feel the pang of losing Frieda, and I am so sad knowing that she could have had an experience such as I have had to have given a richness to the years she had."

"Unless you poisoned the cake, you are stuck with me for while. You know enough about the business by now to carry on with it. The dogs and our friends will keep you whole."

"Nice try, but it would not nearly be the same. It would be better if one of us has to go that I go first."

"For you, maybe, but not for me."

"This is a happy day. Let's not be morbid. Plus, neither one of us can go until our thinking is finished. At the rate we are going, that's a long way off." She reached for his hand, and it was warm and soft as always. That was reassurance enough for now.

TWENTY-ONE

Accustomed to and expecting the bird's presence on the fence, it was disconcerting on a day when it did not appear. It had been five years that the bird had been there at least once during the day even in snow, rain, and high winds. The professor, who knew so much about many things, had said that small birds live on average for two years but that there have been noted incidents where they have lived much longer than that.   They fall prey to larger birds and other adversities. Had the bird died? Was his thinking finished?

It struck Naomi even harder than it did Gil. The bird was her vision of acceptance to the mountains and to this sort of life. It also symbolized the continuance of their personal relationship. It was a pure and simple emotional reaction. Deep down she was assured of the love they shared. That actually was the underpinning for her belonging in this place and time.

Each pass by the side window when they were in the house brought a check to see if the bird had returned. When they were outside, they would peek around the side of the building. Three days later when Gillian was out front he walked to the corner of the building to check. What he saw he was totally unprepared for. There were four birds on the fence. As quietly as he could, he whispered to Naomi who was sweeping the porch at the other end to come over. She gasped at what she saw.

The four birds showed up each day, staying for a few hours each time. As they interpreted it, the row of birds lent new significance to the fence itself. It accentuated that the fence itself did not have a start or an end; it merely ran the length of a part of the old structure. So, in a sense it too was unfinished.

When Ronnie and Yolanda came to sit for a spell, Ronnie had a stern reaction to the latest development. They were all seated on the porch, coffee cups in hand, when Ronnie offered in his unfettered way, "I may sound exasperated with both of you, and I fully intend to sound that way. You have been carrying on this thinking scenario for far too long. It has gotten to the point where you have birds in your belfry. Thinking is thinking and birds are birds. The only connection between the two is in your imagination, your wanting there to be a connection. Just be glad you can think at all at your age, and be glad you have birds to reflect our peaceful mountain life. I know it is a form of an intellectual game, food for discussion, but frankly enough is enough."

Gil motioned to Yolanda. "Are you of the same mind?"

"Yes, I am afraid to say. It's like going around in circles. There is no end to it."

Gil smiled. "Of course, that's the point of it all. There is no end. Oh well, all along I thought you understood. No more coffee for you two. It has affected your power of reason."

Naomi chimed in, rightly believing that these friends were well-intentioned, "These two old crazies will have to find other sympathetic minds to foist our theories on. Speculating about things that have many possible answers or no answers at all, helps to keep mountain folks sharp so that city customers can't take advantage of us. We don't tire of it, but we can see how others can. No more thinking or birds around you two."

Ronnie's wit matched his wisdom. "This place and you two are for the birds anyway."

After they left, a few passerbys stopped to look. One bought a piece of furniture they had brought out just the day before. It always tickled Gil's fancy when a recent item sold. There is just no way to predict it or what people want badly enough to buy it. All antiques dealers have had the same experience, and it was one of the mysteries that defy a solution. It is also an absorbing fascination of the business.

They had an early supper and then sat out on the porch reading. Dutifully, the dogs lay at their feet sleeping but ready to go to the alert in an instant.

Naomi looked up from the book and glanced at Gil. "I hate to say it, but they are right."

"We've known that all along. But, it is one of or favorite games even if we are the only ones playing. Besides, isn't it a part of eccentricity to find symbols in the things that surround us?"

"For now, sure. However, as can be seen it is easy for others to conclude we have gone off the deep end."

"So be it. It enhances our image and mystique."

The cake that Naomi had made had cooled by now. She was glad she learned some helpful tips while doing the stint at the bakery during Ruth's recovery. She went in and cut two large pieces that they could have with the coffee.

Gil took a bite, the anticipation easily satisfied. "Not bad for a gal from Brooklyn. I bet you never thought you would ever bake a mountain cake?"

"You're right. I also only heard about mountain men in relation to myths. Now I know both are real and worth the price."

"What price?"

"The whole shootin' match."

He covered her hand with his and smiled. Even his cake of life now had a bird on it.......a Brooklyn angel.

TWENTY-TWO

It was a brutally hot summer. People flocked to the mountains for some relief. It was hot during the day, but as soon as the sun went down it cooled off. There had been no great need for air conditioning either in the store or the living quarters, although both agreed it would have been nice right now. Added to the heat was a regional serious drought, and many of the smaller streams in the mountains disappeared. People were becoming concerned about wells drying up. It has long been known that adversity brings out either the best or worst in people. Tempers ran short and civility waned even more than it had been in the normal course of events.

Leslie and Harriet still stopped on the way to their cabin. They enjoyed talking to Naomi, and they still brought with them some gourmet item for them to taste. Their Yorkshire Terriers seemed unfazed by time or heat. Morgan and Molly naturally took over Andy's role in looking over them. The river was very low and there would be no canoe riding now. This time, they also stopped as they returned to the city early. Visibly distraught, they told Gil and Naomi that their cabin had been badly vandalized. Windows were broken, the contents smashed and thrown around, and the canoe had a large hole poked through it. Yellow paint was used to scrawl "QUEERS" on one of the walls.

Gillian and Naomi tried their best to calm the pair although it was obvious they were shaken to the point that future visits would never be the same. Naomi was particularly upset. She had no tolerance for evilness of any sort.

Unfortunately, bad events began unraveling. For as long as local residents could remember, there had been little crime, although some minor incidents popped up once and awhile. Criminal activities, some violent in nature, were reported now throughout the region. Perhaps, the vision Ruth had expressed early on that there were so many evil persons emerging in society that no one and nowhere would be safe was prophetic. It seemed as if everywhere one turned there were stories of vandalism and other crimes, many of an aggravated nature. There had been two armed robberies in town. A violent home invasion had taken place near the county line. A real estate agent had been assaulted. The Sheriff's office issued a dire warning and urged great caution by all.

Even isolated as they were, they refused to be fearful. Morgan and Molly were better than any alarm system. Gil never had or used a personal firearm. He did not believe in their use, even for hunting. One of the causes that Ronnie had urged him to join was the unpopular movement for absolute gun control.

Even though the heat wave was relentless, the crime reports kept many tourists away from seeking relief in the mountains. Reduced business activity added more uneasiness throughout the community. Life in the mountains is tourist driven.

Fewer cars came down the highway this steamy summer day. Naomi was tidying up in the living quarters after a light lunch. Gil parked himself in a rocker on the porch with the dogs at his feet. Before sitting he had peeked around the corner of the building to make sure the birds were rightfully perched. The heat probably was not a burden to the birds, and the fence was shaded by the large trees.

The rocker was an old friend, and Gil always felt relaxed in it. He knew he would doze off shortly. First, his active mind led him in an entirely different direction. His absorption with unfinished thinking had been on an individual basis. Now, his focus shifted to a larger picture. There had to be unfinished thinking on the societal level as well. This new mental direction was prompted by the increasing existence of violent acts. It defied the logic and deep meaning of the nation's history. He thought of all of the lives lost in war battles fought to preserve the freedoms we all have. Those promising lives, many who might have become great leaders and achievers for a better world, lost to afford contrarians and extremists an opportunity to display their hate. Those that violently pronounce disgust with the values of the nation, add disgrace to those who died for the country. Laws can provide punishment, but what can be done to make sense in an increasingly senseless world?

Naomi came out to join him. "Quiet today, too quiet. I am surprised to see you are still awake,"

"I am worried about our mountain existence as well as the future of the country."

"I am as well. Now that I have a life that I cherish, I feel it is threatened."

"In a nation of justice and peace, much of life is jeopardized by constant worry for safety."

Naomi wiped the perspiration from her brow. "I am not going to live worrying about being beaten or killed. I am not going to let anything or anyone detract from our precious moments. What happens will happen, and we will deal with it whatever comes along."

"That sounds mighty eccentric to me."

"I have a good teacher." She reached out and covered his hand with her fingers.

Naomi went in and brought out two glasses of iced lemonade that she had made before lunch. Gil was sound asleep. She drank both glasses before she shut her eyes.

As soon as they were sure both were asleep, Morgan and Molly closed their eyes. Their world was untroubled. Perhaps there is some lesson in that.

TWENTY-THREE

The weeks of summer glided by. Cooler temperatures and frequent rains that broke the drought and the violent incidents ended as quickly as they had emerged. Tourism rose accordingly, and business at the shop was brisk. As a component of unfinished thinking, seeking explanations for certain whys and wherefores could be puzzling.

Early one morning they had a surprise visit from Pastor Tom and his wife, Martha. Tom had offered to marry them when that event was decided upon, but he accepted the decision opting for a civil ceremony since Naomi was Jewish. Tom and Martha stopped by occasionally and conversation was casual and friendly. Tom had a keen sense of humor and was at his best relating a funny story. Today, his mission was apparently of a more serious nature.

After a bout of small talk, Tom addressed the concern that had brought on this visit. "Being a pastor is like being a shepherd looking after his flock. Trouble brews when one of the sheep wanders away. I think the hardest thing I do these days and the most time-consuming is not instilling and perpetuating faith in the Lord, rather it is trying to hold families together. Marriage is a far cry from what it used to be, and the family unit is weak and often splintered. I do more visits to broken homes than to folks who are in the hospital or otherwise not well or to generate interest in the church. A particularly heart-wrenching situation involved Fred and Iris Conners who lived at the other end of the county. I do not know if you knew them or heard what happened."

Gil shook his head. Tom continued, "I get choked up just thinking about it. Martha, why don't you tell the rest."

Martha put her glass down on the covered barrel next to the rocker that served as a table. "Tom suffers as much as the participants in a tragedy. The Conners came to church regularly. Nine years ago when they were going to the grocery store their car skidded on a sheet of ice on old 420 and slammed into a tree. They died, but their six-year-old daughter, Belinda, who was in the back seat survived. Her left arm was pinned under the car, and by the time they got her to the hospital the arm had to be removed. The Conners had no relatives able or willing to take Belinda. She has been in foster homes for nine years, the foster families not keeping her as she became more and more rowdy and rebellious. Now, at age fifteen, no one wants a one-armed behavioral problem. We thought that you two, being around all of the time and with a stable home situation, might consider taking her in. We would do it ourselves if we could, but our health is taking a beating and Tom may soon have to give up preaching."

Tom interjected, "We hate to thrust this on you, but this might be her last chance at a normal life."

Gillian and Naomi exchanged glances. Gil took a long sip of the yellowish liquid, the ice cubes clanking against the glass. "That is quite a story. I think I speak for Naomi too when I say we are in no financial situation to take on this kind of added responsibility not to mention the limited space we have here."

Tom interrupted him, "The State pays for fostering."

Naomi joined in. "Neither one of us has any parenting experience or skills."

Martha smiled. "Being a parent comes from the will. Besides, Belinda is fifteen and not really a child. If you treat her as an adult she will undoubtedly respond that way."

Gil chimed in, hoping the tone of annoyance was not as obvious as he felt it. "We are basically too old and set in our ways to tackle this. It represents a total upheaval to our existence."

"I know this is much to thrust on you," Tom was solemn. "You don't have to answer right now. Think about it. A soul, a lost soul, is at stake here."

After Tom and Martha left, a steady stream of customers came in. That was probably a good thing because it gave them time to sort out their thoughts before an inevitable discussion.

Naomi made sandwiches and they ate out on the porch. Molly and Morgan had been fed and quickly fell asleep after being alert the whole time customers were around.

They were silent while they ate, but even the birds on the fence were anticipating a lively discussion. Naomi spoke first. "Talk about unfinished thinking! I am not sure we will agree on this but I think we should meet Belinda and take it from there. I always wondered what it was like to have a child, and maybe this is a chance to find out. It would bring all kinds of challenges neither one of us has ever anticipated, and I do not want anything to infringe on our life together. You know that."

Gil did not respond right away. "I suppose I feel the same way, but we cannot make a totally emotional decision. We need to be practical. I fear it would be biting off more than we can chew. If it is more of a strain than satisfaction, is it worth it? We are talking about a person. If we bought an antique that turned out to be a bad investment, we would know the extent of our loss. How do you measure investing in the present and future days of a child who may resent or hate what we may want to do? We have a calm life together. Do we want to jeopardize that by injecting an unknown into the equation?"

"Right. But, that is only one side. What if we can guide her to a happy and useful life? Wouldn't that be reward enough?"

Gil reached for her hand. Their fingers comfortably intertwined. "Let's sleep on it. In the morning we'll consult with Molly and Morgan just in case we all need to vote on it."

TWENTY-FOUR

There are intruding times where restlessness dominates over weariness when in potential sleep mode. Such a time is when a monumental decision needs to be made. For Gil, it loomed larger than his decision to quit the Raleigh job and move to the mountains. That step was right because nearly everything before that was a form of prelude. For Naomi, it clearly had greater consequences than when she opted to ask Gil to take her to the mountains with him. If he had declined, she would have been no worse off than if she had not asked him at all. Here, there was a slew of considerations and unknowns that would boggle any mind, especially an old mind. Murky waters clouded what a decision would usher in. There was no assurance of a right choice.

It was a beautiful day for late summer, and they lingered on the porch sipping their second cup of coffee. The birds were ensconced on the fence and the dogs dutifully laying at their feet, so all seemed just right with the world for the moment. This was both reassuring and disquieting as change was at stake.

From the poor sleep, Gil felt tired. Normally, a nap would be in order but not today. "I remember Jack telling me that he once came across a crystal ball that a fortune teller had used. That would sure come in handy right now."

"It probably would," Naomi chuckled, "But putting our two minds together should produce a more realistic prediction."

"Is it just the mind? What about the heart? I keep telling myself that I am so eccentric that the sensible solution is out of whack."

"And what is the sensible solution?"

"To leave well enough alone."

"So you basically think we should go ahead with this. I lean in that direction as well, but I think we should meet Belinda before we decide for sure."

"I have the feeling that once we meet her it will be too late to retreat."

"Probably. But, we won't know anything until it happens."

"You sure are a sweetheart, and I am one lucky guy to have you. Are you really up to all of this?"

"Alone, no. With you, yes."

It was arranged that in three days Pastor Tom would bring Belinda to the shop for a visit and lunch and then would pick her up four hours later. Gil and Naomi debated about closing the shop but opted for keeping things as routine as possible. The girl had to accept them as well and it had to be under normal conditions and behavior.

Belinda was smaller than what they figured a fifteen year old girl should be. She was also frail looking, and the long-sleeved sweater worn on a hot day was baggy and hung limp where her left arm would have been. Dingy short brown hair was unevenly cut, apparently a rush home job. Large brown eyes had a dullness that portrayed annals of a hard life. Thin lips neither spoke nor smiled.

Gil figured that on top of everything else she probably had never seen a long-bearded old crazy man before, so he let Naomi do all of the talking and showing her around. Belinda seemed disinterested in it all, and the few words she uttered in a raspy voice were in a monotone. The first half smile came when they sat in the rockers on the porch when Morgan came to her and put his chin on her leg. Belinda petted him with her only hand, and then Molly came over for similar attention. At times, animals can do what people are unable to.

Naomi had made little pizzas on English muffins for lunch figuring that would be pleasing to a teenager. Belinda devoured them along with Naomi's famous lemonade. She still did not say much but there was a definite spark in her eyes. Gil surmised it was a reflection of the glimmer in her stomach.

He spoke humorously, "Do you know what foster birds are?"

Belinda shook her head. Gil motioned for her to follow him as they went around the corner of the building. The four sparrows were all in place on the fence. "These are foster birds. We have given them a place to rest and take in all of the activity of the shop. Would you like to be our foster bird?"

Belinda looked at the dogs who had naturally followed them. There was a hint of annoyance in her voice. "I would, but I don't follow orders."

"That's alright cause I don't give orders. There are so many things that need to be done around here that they sort of speak for themselves. If you give it all a chance, the dogs, the birds, and the antiques will all talk to you in a very special way."

Gil could tell that she was sizing up the situation. What he did not know was what she was thinking to herself. *There is so much confusion and junk here I can do what I want when I want. It is going to be good pickings living with these two old farts.*

TWENTY-FIVE

It took a week for the paperwork to be completed and to be effective. They went to pick up Belinda at her present foster home, and she was waiting on the front steps with a small suitcase. Naomi made a mental note to take the girl shopping for clothes. Apparently, she did not have much, and the following week was also the start of the new school year.

They had put that week to good use. A corner area of the living space that had a window was cleared out, and Len put up walls and a door. They found a bed and small desk at Showells' Used Furniture store, and they moved an armoire to be used as a closet from the shop as well as a small antique dresser. It was a bit cramped, but Belinda should have what she needed for comfort and she would have privacy. Sharing the only bathroom might be a problem, but it was hoped that would be the only problem.

Belinda was silent the entire drive home, and they could only guess what she might be thinking. Her face lighted up when she received an enthusiastic greeting from the dogs. She grunted what they interpreted as a form of approval when shown her bedroom. Gil wondered if a day would ever come when the girl would show appreciation for what they were doing for her. Maybe, this will wind up to be a second-guess event, and there had been very few of those in his past.

Belinda had to admit to herself that it will be nice to have a bedroom of her own, even if a bit cramped. There had been few luxuries in her life and she wanted that to change. It did not matter who she had to step on to get them.

There was only one high school in the county, and classes started the next week. They would have to drive her to a bus stop two miles down the road. Naomi wanted her to feel good about school, so she took her to the mall in the next county to get her a special outfit for the first day of school. A trip to the hair salon was in order to style her hair. As Naomi knew too well, even a woman with plain features can look her best and feel good about herself with certain adornments.

Nobody had ever done such things for Belinda before, and she had to admit she liked being with the old woman. She liked the way she talked in such soft tones, and it was interesting when she added flowery phrases to what otherwise would be an ordinary conversation.

The weeks slid by and an early autumn brought an influx of tourists to the mountains. The store was packed at times and Belinda willingly pitched in to help once she mastered the cash register and she was not involved with homework. She wanted to prove to them that she was smart, as it was obvious that the old folks were intellectuals, a kind of people that Belinda had not encountered before. It was not just the massive collection of books, but they knew about things that were not obvious. She liked to roam through the books. At first, she was attracted to the pretty books and then her interest shifted to captivating titles. There was so much to learn and she set her mind to fulfill that endeavor.

After determining that the old folks kept poor sales records and just how much money was coming in, each time she opened the register the cash was tantalizing. She could take some and nobody would be the wiser. That might come in handy at some point.

The birds on the fence took on a special significance for Belinda. It was reassuring to see them perched there most of the time. For a person who was purposely shifted from place to place, it came to represent a form of continuity and permanence. Gil had explained to her the idea of unfinished thinking, but that was a bunch of gibberish. Old folks had a tendency to run their thoughts together so that it was confusing to a youngster accustomed to dealing with one idea at a time. No wonder no one understood them or wanted to understand them. While she had no friends and felt comfortable being a loner, to her there was a vast difference between a young person choosing to go it alone and old persons who were forced to be in their own world because nobody else cared to be part of it with them. She knew she would be old some day, and would probably wind up to be as eccentric as they claimed to be, but there was a great time and space between the now and the then and she intended to live every minute the way that she thought it ought to be. The one thing she knew for sure was that she would have dogs. She loved Molly and Morgan and soaked up their nonjudgmental love for her.

Gil and Naomi were able to talk freely about Belinda when she was in school. Gil was still not convinced they had done the right thing taking her in. "You know I do not care what a person looks like, and she may find it is a disadvantage to be ordinary, yet I do not think she recognizes what we are trying to do for her."

"Ordinary is only skin deep. We are living examples of that. She has had a hard life, and it will take time for her potential to surface. We need to be patient while she sorts things out. I believe she will come around. I just wish she would be more loving. I suppose I always pictured a child that way. She has the capacity. I see it when she is with the dogs."

"The dogs are not a threat to her. We are because we can exercise control over her."

"As long as she is wary of us she cannot love us."

"She is surrounded by loving examples. If she were younger, it might be easier to fall in with it. She is almost a woman and her frame of reference is particularly different. By the time she is eighteen and legally on her own, she'll either be part of us or leave us. I suppose that is a different kind of unfinished thinking."

Naomi embraced him. "There are too many loose ends for an old woman to be completely content."

He pressed her to him strongly, noting their breathing was in unison. "Babe, we take what we can get."

TWENTY-SIX

Coincidentally, the first snow fell on Belinda's sixteenth birthday. The schools were closed and the unplowed roads meant no customers that day. Ruth had brought a birthday cake out the day before when she heard the forecast. It looked like it would be a long and leisurely celebration of the occasion. They had bought Belinda a computer as a birthday present, and she would no longer have to struggle with the early model Naomi had brought from Brooklyn. A computer does not know the person operating it has only one hand.

Belinda was truly surprised. It was a gift that reached to her heart. She had not received many generous outpourings in the hard life that had been imposed on her. Yet, in the brief time she had been with this unusual couple, she learned to accept their kindness and concern. She liked the way they affectionately interacted and she was now quick to seek their guidance and advice. They were different from other adults she had encountered, and even in a consistent wariness she felt a growing connection to them. They were different and she was different. It made little sense but there was a natural fit. She knew she could and wanted to love as it was easy to love the dogs. Now, she looked forward to the outlandish things these old folks would say and do, and a respect evolved into an admiration and the kind of love she felt for the dogs. Most of the school crowd found her physical condition grotesque and they avoided her and made fun of her. She could take that. Here, she was experiencing a warm home environment with no forced togetherness. She no longer thought in terms of taking advantage of the old folks. They demanded nothing from her and asked for little. Who would not thrive in those conditions?

At the sight of the computer, Belinda hugged them. It was the first display of affection, and it was a welcome surprise. In this relatively brief time, they had noticed her emotional and social progress. It reaffirmed the decision they had made to adopt Belinda. When they told her of that decision, an additional warm hug came quickly.

Naomi would select a book that she thought Belinda might enjoy and lead to a love of reading. It was left on the youngster's desk, and she thought it was a fun game. It certainly worked, and Belinda read every chance she had, and would throw out torrents of questions to the adults as ideas prompted them. Her interest and involvement with the antiques grew once she realized that objects have stories just as people. She chipped in with cleaning shelves and items, and the growing curiosity led to question after question.

Each day seemed to bring a new challenge and accomplishment of parenthood, especially as to a teenager. A monumental upheaval came in the spring when Belinda was asked out on her first date. She had made a friend at school, Blake Champton, who also had only one arm. He had lost an arm in a freak accident six years ago when he was helping his father on their farm. The common handicap served as an initial common bond which grew to a close friendship and partnership to ward off the thoughtless and mean comments by others.

Blake's father drove the couple to the mall in the next county where there was a movie complex. He waited for them and after the movie took them to an ice cream parlor where he let them sit in private. When Belinda was dropped off the excitement that had emerged prior to the actual date had not waned and probably was even greater because Blake had kissed her goodnight. It was well after the normal bedtime of the older folks but it was hard not to get swept up in the fervor of the moment. Even Molly and Morgan were jumping around.

It took awhile for a relative calm to take hold, and eventually everyone went to bed. Gil was the only one who could not sleep. The mind of an old man once in overdrive takes a prolonged period to settle down. He slipped out of Naomi's loving embrace and went out on the porch. Even though it was late spring, a chill was in the air. He zipped up his jacket and sat in a rocker.

Gil was getting a fresh insight concerning the unfinished thinking scenario. Ronnie had been fairly close to the gist of it when he had thrown out as one of the possibilities of unfinished thinking as being just a personal demon, a gnawing feeling that Gil was not totally who he was meant to be and that a vital element in his life was still out there to be claimed. That had also been his initial reaction as the concept took a prominent place in his outlook. Yet, it went beyond that. He had built nearly the entire foundation of his life on a form of eccentricity. The realization came rushing in that perhaps he was not as eccentric as he made himself out to be. Two so-called normal developments had caused him to rein in his wild steed. The first was finding an abiding love with Naomi. The love he felt for this woman was as strong as any emotion he had in his entire lifetime. She was an exceptionally good, kind, and caring person. Her feelings and reactions were sincere. If a person was pure in the sense of being uncomplicated and genuine, it was Naomi. There were no pretenses, no coveting of unrealistic or impractical rewards, no measuring of taking before giving. That alone had seeped in to fill any void in his life. It were the voids, he realized, that was his unfinished thinking. The second reality was the entry in his heart of a child that he suspected would not be anywhere near as a perfect person. Yet, a whole body was not a deterrent to a complete person. He had an overwhelming urge to nurture and protect her, and that urge was probably more for him than it was for her. And, whether she ever grew to love him as he now loved her was not the crucial lesson. It was this untapped capacity for additional love of a child that he discovered was important to the completeness of him as a person. Too bad he was so enlightened at such an old age. If his death came, he was ready for it. His thinking was finished. His life was complete. He hoped he might enjoy the fruits of the harvest for some years to come, but he was assured that he would be his own person until the end.

Morgan licked his hand, and he realized in the early light of a new day that he had slept in the rocker all night. Naomi was holding a cup of coffee and offering it to him. She kissed him on the forehead and sat in the adjoining rocker with a coffee of her own. It was as sweet a moment as any old man could rightfully ask for.

www.ingramcontent.com/pod-product-compliance
Lightning Source LLC
Chambersburg PA
CBHW031846170626
46807CB00004B/1650